D0553457

Karnak Café

Karnak Café

Naguib Mahfouz

Translated by Roger Allen

The American University in Cairo Press
Cairo New York

First published in 2007 by
The American University in Cairo Press
113 Sharia Kasr el Aini, Cairo, Egypt
420 Fifth Avenue, New York 10018
www.aucpress.com

Dar el Kutub No. 23343/06
ISBN-10: 977 416 072 X
ISBN-13: 978 977 416 072 1

1 2 3 4 5 6   12 11 10 09 08 07

Designed by Sally Boylan/AUC Press Design Center
Printed in Egypt

❧ Qurunfula ❧

I t was sheer chance that brought me to the Karnak
Café. One day I'd made my way to al-Mahdi Street to
get my watch repaired; the job was going to take several hours, so I had to wait. To kill the time I decided to look
at all the watches, jewelry, and trinkets on display in the
store windows on both sides of the street. And that's how I
came to stumble across the café.

It's very small and off the main street. Since that day it's
become my favorite place to sit and pass the time. To tell
you the truth, at first I hesitated by the entrance for a
moment, but then I spotted a woman sitting on a stool by
the cash register, the usual spot for the manageress. You
could tell she was getting old, and yet she still had vestiges
of her former beauty. Those clear, refined features of hers
jogged something buried deep in my memory. All of a sudden the images came flooding back. I could hear music and
drums. I was sitting there watching a gorgeous body swaying
from side to side; the air was permeated by the aroma of
incense. A dancer, that's what she was. Yes, the star of 'Imad
al-Din, none other than Qurunfula herself! Now there she

was sitting on the stool, Qurunfula in person, the roseate dream from the 1940s.

So that was how I came to enter the Karnak Café. I felt drawn in by some obscure magic force and a carefree heart, and all because of someone who had never even heard of me. We had never had any kind of relationship, whether of affection, self-interest, or simply courtesy. At one time she had been a real star, whereas I was just one of her contemporaries. The admiring glances that I directed at her still-glorious figure seemed to have absolutely no effect on her, and I did not feel I had any reason to go over and say hello. So I just took a seat and started looking around the café.

It seemed to consist simply of one large room, but it was all neat and tidy. There was wallpaper on the walls, and the chairs and tables looked new; mirrors all around and colored lamps as well. The plates, dishes, and cups looked clean. All in all, its attractions as a place to sit were pretty irresistible. Every time the opportunity arose, I stared long and hard at Qurunfula. The bewitching femininity of her earlier days was long gone, of course, along with the bloom of youth, but in their place there was an enigmatic kind of beauty, accentuated by a sorrowful expression that touched your heart. Her body was still lithe and svelte, and gave the impression that she could still be lively and energetic when need be. And with it all there was a sense of a carefully controlled inner strength, the result of many years of experience and work. The carefree mood that she exuded was totally captivating. Her glances would take in the entire establishment and kept the wine-steward, waiter, and cleaner on their toes. For the relatively few regulars at the café she showed tremendous affection; the place was so small that they all seemed like a single family. There were three old men who may have been in retirement, another middle-aged man, and a group of younger people, including a very pretty girl.

All this made me feel out of place. I certainly was feeling happy enough, but still I got the impression that somehow I was intruding. Good God, I told myself, I really like this place. The coffee is excellent, the water is pure, and the cups and glasses are models of cleanliness. Beyond that, there's that sweetness about Qurunfula, the respectability of those old men, and the lively atmosphere that those young people over there bring in, not to mention the pretty girl. It's right in the middle of the big city, just the place for a wanderer like me to relax for a while. Here you get to sense past and present in a warm embrace, the sweet past and glorious present. To top it all, there is that enticement that the unknown brings. There I was, needing to have my watch repaired, and now I find myself succumbing to a multi-faceted infatuation! Very well then, Karnak Café can be my haven of rest and relaxation whenever time permits.

At that moment I had a very agreeable surprise. Qurunfula apparently decided to walk over and welcome me as a new customer. She left her chair and came toward me. She was wearing dark blue slacks and a white blouse.

"I'm pleased to see you here," she said, standing right in front of me.

We shook hands, and I thanked her for her welcome.

"Did you like the coffee?" she asked.

"Very much," I replied truthfully, "an excellent blend."

She smiled contentedly and stared at me for a moment. "I get the impression," she went on, "that you remember me from before. Am I right?"

"Yes," I replied, "who could ever forget Qurunfula?"

"But can you remember what I really did for art?"

"Certainly, you were the first to modernize belly dancing."

"Have you ever heard or read about anyone who acknowledges that fact?"

"Sometimes nations are afflicted with a corporate loss of memory," I replied, feeling awkward, "but it never lasts for ever."

"That's all very well," she replied, "but those are empty words."

"To the contrary, what I just said is absolutely true." I was eager to get out of this tight corner, so I went on, "I wish you a very happy life. That's what's most important."

She laughed. "Thus far," she said, "the conclusion seems to be a happy one." With that she turned away and went back to her chair, but not before she bade me farewell with the words, "But only God knows the unseen!"

So we got to know each other; it was that simple. It turned into a new friendship, one that gave me then and has continued to give me much pleasure. It was new in one sense, and yet behind it there were other features that went back thirty years or more. Our meetings and conversations continued and indeed blossomed till a bond of genuine affection was established.

One day it occurred to me that she may have been a brilliant and gorgeous dancer, yet at the same time she had always been respectable.

"You were a wonderful dancer," I told her, "but you still managed to keep your respectability. Wasn't that some kind of miracle?"

"Before me belly dancing involved the three b's: belly, bosom, and buttocks," she responded proudly. "I turned it into something more tasteful."

"How did you manage that?"

"I made sure never to miss the dancing soirees at al-Bargula." She shook her head suggestively. "On the matter of respectability," she went on, "I made it a matter of public knowledge that I would never consent to any relationship which didn't involve genuine love, nor would I make love with anyone if there was no question of marriage."

"And that was it?" I asked in amazement.

"If respectability has a public face," she replied with a laugh, "that's enough, isn't it?"

I nodded in agreement. She muttered something that I couldn't hear, then continued, "True love will always give a relationship a legitimacy that is hard to fault."

"So that's why no magazine ever dragged your name through the mud."

"That's right, not even the worst of them."

"Even so, there were a lot of men whose lives went downhill over you."

"Yes," she replied with a sigh, "nightlife is filled with personal tragedies."

"I can still remember the tale of that Finance Ministry official."

"Shhhh!" she interrupted with a whisper. "Do you mean 'Arif Sulayman? He's over there, just a few yards away from you. He's the steward behind the bar!"

I sneaked a look in his direction as he stood there in his usual spot. He looked paunchy, and his hair had turned white; his expression was downtrodden and submissive.

Qurunfula obviously noticed how astonished I looked. "It's not the way you imagine," she said. "He wasn't a victim of mine; he was a victim of his own weakness."

With that she told me a story that sounded quite normal. He had been absolutely crazy about her, but she had never given him the slightest encouragement. He had never had enough money to hang around the dancehall all the time, so he had started dipping his hand into the state's coffers. Among all the other customers he had looked like some rich heir, but she had never taken a single penny from him. The only relationship they had had was firmly based on the regulations and traditions of nightclubs. But matters had not proceeded very far before he was caught red-handed; he had been taken to court and given a prison sentence.

"It was a tragedy, sure enough," she said, "but it wasn't my fault. Years later he came out of prison. He showed up at the very same nightclub and told me that his life was in ruins. I felt sorry for the man and not a little anxious as well. I spoke to the club owner on his behalf and got him a job as a waiter. Once I stopped dancing and opened this café, I decided to hire him as wine-steward. He does a very good job."

"Didn't his old infatuation sometimes get the better of him?" I asked, stroking my moustache.

"Oh yes, it did," she replied. "When he was a waiter at the nightclub, he kept on harassing me. That got him a really nasty beating. At the time I was married to a real elephant of a man who was a champion weight lifter. One year later, he married a dancer in one of the theater troupes; they're still married and have seven daughters. Today I think he's happy and successful enough. . . ." With that she dissolved into laughter. "These days we occasionally decide to exchange a love-kiss."

"Thus is the past forgotten."

"Then it happened that one of his former colleagues got an unexpected promotion to the rank of under-secretary in the Finance Ministry. That made him feel a real sense of grievance; he wanted to take revenge on the entire world. However, along came the 1952 Revolution, and his ex-colleague was pensioned off. With that he calmed down a lot and became one of the revolution's great admirers."

I became part of the Karnak Café family. The entire group felt like an integral part of me. Qurunfula gave me her friendship, and I reciprocated. She used to play backgammon with the old men: Muhammad Bahgat, Rashad Magdi, and Taha al-Gharib. I also made the acquaintance of the young folk, especially Zaynab Diyab, Isma'il al-Shaykh, and Hilmi Hamada. I also met Zayn al-'Abidin 'Abdallah, who was public relations director at some company or other. Even Imam al-Fawwal, the waiter, and Gum'a, the bootblack and sweeper, became friends of mine. I discovered the secret

7

behind the economics of Karnak Café: it didn't need to rely on the limited number of customers who came in, instead it counted on the owners and customers of the various taverns on al-Mahdi Street. That was why the drinks at the café were so good, in fact exceptional. There was another secret about the café too, namely that it was—and still is—a gathering-place for people with extremely interesting and provocative viewpoints; whether they yell or speak softly, they are expressing the realities of living history. Ever since I became a member of their company, the numerous conversations I've had there have been unforgettable, as has Qurunfula's own sense of gratitude every time she has intoned, "Thank God who has brought us the revolution!"

Both 'Arif Sulayman, the wine-steward, and Zayn al-'Abidin, the public relations director, were fervent admirers of the revolution as well, each of them in his own particular way and for his own purposes. As far as the old men were concerned, they too were equally enthusiastic for the revolution, but they did occasionally introduce another note into the conversation: "The past wasn't all that bad," they would say with a properly nuanced caution.

The young folk used to gather in a corner; from it, bursts of enthusiasm would emerge with a great roar. As far as they were concerned, history began with the 1952 Revolution. Everything before then was some obscure and inexplicable "period of ignorance." They were the real children of the revolution. But for its achievements, they would all have been loitering around the streets and alleys with no real sense of purpose. From time to time we would hear hints of opposition that suggested either the views of the extreme left or else a cautious mention under the breath of an affiliation with the Muslim Brotherhood. However, such ideas would soon be lost in the general hubbub. I was particularly struck by Imam al-Fawwal, the waiter, and Gum'a, the bootblack. Both of them used to complain about how hard their life was, and yet they could both burst into song in praise of the great pre-Islamic cavalier, 'Antar, and his various conquests; it was as if references to victory, honor, and hope could somehow make their poverty easier to bear.

Actually, everyone was eager to share this feeling of elation, even those whose hearts were being eaten up by envy and hatred. All the people sitting there inside the café had buried deep inside them some kind of bitter experience, whether humiliation, defeat, or failure. Their craving for a full glass would inspire them to challenge all their former foes. They would drink to the very dregs and then start dancing for the sheer joy of it. What's the point of criticizing something with a whole load of drunks around? Bribery, you say? Pilfering, corruption, coercion, terrorism? Shit! Or, so what? Or, it's an inevitable evil. Or, how utterly trivial. Come on, take another swig from the magic glass, and let's dance together.

Whenever Qurunfula gets back from the hairdresser, she looks really beautiful. Her honey-colored eyes sparkle. On one occasion this prompted me to ask her a question: "Aren't you married any more? Don't you have any children?"

9

She didn't say anything, and I immediately regretted letting the question slip. For her part, she noticed that I was embarrassed.

"See these people?" she said, pointing at the customers. "I love them, and they love me."

Just then for no apparent reason she whispered to herself the words, "Love, love."

"We all had good times being in love with the people we loved," she went on sadly, "but the only thing that lingers is a sense of disappointment."

"Disappointment?"

"Yes, disappointment. That's what happens to a love that manages to escape from reality's clutches, only to linger on as a tantalizing hope."

"Have you ever been disappointed in love?" I asked discreetly.

"No, not exactly," she replied, "but sometimes love plays the coquette with you."

"But not in your glory days, surely?"

"Oh, it can happen any time."

I was eager to hear more, but she decided to ignore my obvious curiosity. She spotted Zayn al-'Abidin out of the corner of her eye.

"Just look at him," she continued. "He's in love with me. What does he want? He's suggested that we go into partnership with the café and turn it into a restaurant. But what he's really after is to get me into bed with him."

"But the man's so old, he's preserved in oil!"

"Impossible dreams!"

"He might be rich, of course."

"The state's money. That's the place you need to look for your blessings."

I looked toward 'Arif Sulayman, the wine-steward. It was a completely unconscious gesture, but she still noticed.

"He pilfered money for love's sake," she said. "But Zayn al-'Abidin grabs it out of sheer greed and ambition. My dear, it takes all types. . . . Some people take merely in order to stay alive because the government doesn't provide for them; others are simply greedy; still others are on the take because everyone else is doing the same thing. And while all these people are carrying on like that, the poor young people trapped in the middle go crazy."

"So now we're back to our original point," I said with some emphasis.

"You realize that I'm in love, don't you?" she asked me forthrightly.

True enough, I had noticed certain things, but now she had caught me red-handed.

"You're no fool," she said, "so don't even ask me who it is."

"Hilmi Hamada?" I inquired with a smile.

Without even excusing herself she made her way back to her chair; once there she threw me the sweetest of smiles. At one time I had thought it was Isma'il al-Shaykh, but then I discovered that he and Zaynab Diyab were very close. After that things had become clearer. Hilmi Hamada was a very trim and handsome young man, always very excitable when there was an argument. Qurunfula was quite frank with me. She had been the one to make the amorous overtures, in fact right in front of his young friends. On one occasion she was sitting next to him and listening to him speak his mind about some political controversy: "Long live everything you want to live," she yelled, "and death to anyone you want to see dead!"

She invited him up to her apartment on the fourth floor of the building (the café was on the first floor). Once there she gave him a sumptuous welcome. The sitting room was decked with flowers, there was a huge spread on the table, and dance music was playing on the tape recorder.

"He loves me too," she told me confidently, "you can be quite sure of that." She paused for a short while, then continued in a more serious tone, "But actually he has no idea how much I love him." Then there was a flash of anger. "One of these days I expect he'll just get up and leave for good . . . but then, what else is new?" That last phrase came out with a shrug of the shoulders.

"You're aware of everything, and yet you still insist on going your own way."

"That's a pretty fatuous remark, but it might just as well serve as a motto for life itself."

"On behalf of the living," I commented with a smile, "allow me to thank you."

"But Hilmi's serious and generous too. He was the first person to get enthusiastic about my project."

"And which project might that be, if you please?"

"Writing my memoirs. I'm absolutely crazy about the idea. The only thing holding me back is that I'm no good at writing."

"Is he helping you write them down on a regular basis?"

"Yes, he is. And he's very keen about it too."

"So he's interested in art and history?"

"That's one side of it. Other parts deal with the secret lives of Egypt's men and women."

"People from the previous generation?"

"The present one as well."

"You mean, scandals and things like that?"

"Once in a while there's a reference to some scandals, but I have more worthwhile goals than just that."

"It sounds risky," I said, introducing a note of caution.

"There'll be an uproar when it's published," she went on with a mixture of pride and concern.

"You mean, if it is ever published," I commented with a laugh.

She gave me a frown. "The first part can be published with no problems."

"Fine. Then I'd leave the second part to be published in the fullness of time."

"My mother lived till she was ninety," she responded hopefully.

"And may God grant you a long life too, Qurunfula," I said, in the same hopeful tone.

There came a day when I arrived at the café only to find all the chairs normally occupied by the young people empty. The entire place looked very odd, and a heavy silence hung over everything. The old men were busy playing backgammon and

13

chatting, but Qurunfula kept casting anxious glances toward the door. She came over and sat down beside me.

"None of them have come," she said. "What can have happened?"

"Maybe they had an appointment somewhere else."

"All of them? He might have let me know, even if it was just a phone call."

"I don't think there's anything to worry about."

"Perhaps not," she said sharply, "but there's plenty to be angry about."

Evening turned into night, but none of them showed up. The following evening it was the same story. Qurunfula's mood changed, and she became a bundle of nerves, going in and out of the café.

"How do you explain it all?" she asked.

I shook my head in despair.

"Oh, they're just youngsters," was Zayn al-'Abidin's contribution to the conversation. "They never stay anywhere for too long. They've gone somewhere else that suits them better."

Qurunfula lost her temper and rounded on him. "What a stupid idiot you are!" she said. "Why don't you go somewhere that suits you better as well?"

"Oh no," he replied with an imbecilic laugh, "I'm already in the most suitable place."

At this point I did my best to smooth things over. "I'm sure we'll see them again at any moment."

"The worry of it all is killing me," she whispered in my ear.

"Don't you know where he lives?" I asked delicately.

"No, I don't," she replied. "It's somewhere in the Husayniya Quarter. He's a medical student, but the college is closed for summer vacation. As you can tell, I've no idea where he lives."

Days and weeks passed, and Qurunfula almost went out of her mind. I joined her in her sorrow.

"You're destroying yourself," I told her. "Have a little pity, at least on yourself."

"It's not pity I need," she replied. "It's him."

Zayn al-'Abidin avoided any further tirades by saying nothing and keeping his thoughts to himself. Actually, he was feeling profoundly happy about the new situation, but he managed to keep his true feelings hidden by looking glum and puffing away on his shisha.

One day Taha al-Gharib spoke up. "I hear there have been widespread arrests."

No one said a word. After this moment of loaded silence I thought I would try to be as helpful as possible. "But these young folk all support the revolution," I said.

That led Rashad Magdi to insert his opinion. "And there's a not inconsiderable minority of them who oppose it."

"It's quite clear what's happened," Muhammad Bahgat suggested. "They decided to put the guilty ones in prison, so they've dragged all the friends in too. That way the investigation will be complete."

Qurunfula kept following this conversation. The expression on her face was one of utter confusion, and it made her look almost stupid. She adamantly refused either to understand or be convinced by anything she was hearing.

15

Meanwhile the conversation continued with everyone contributing their own ideas about what was happening.

"Imprisonment is really scary."

"The things you hear about what's being done to prisoners are even more scary."

"Rumors like those are enough to make your stomach churn."

"There's no judicial hearing and no defense."

"There's no legal code in the first place!"

"But people keep saying that we're living through a revolutionary process that requires the use of extraordinary measures like these."

"Yes, and they go on to say that we all have to sacrifice freedom and the rule of law, but only for a short while."

"But this revolution is thirteen years old and more. Surely it's about time things settled down and became more stable."

Qurunfula started neglecting her job. She would spend all or part of the day somewhere else; sometimes she didn't appear for twenty-four hours at a stretch. It would be left to 'Arif Sulayman and Imam al-Fawwal to run the café.

When she reappeared, she used to tell us that she had been to see all the influential people she knew from both past and present. She had asked them all for information, but nobody knew anything. "What you keep getting," she told us, "are totally unexpected remarks, like 'How are we supposed to know,' or 'I'd be careful about asking too many questions,' or even worse, 'If I were you, I wouldn't offer any young folk hospitality in your café!' What on earth has happened to the world?"

With that my own thoughts went off on an entirely new
tack, the primary impulse being a feeling of profound sadness.
Yes indeed, I told myself, this life we're living does have its
painful and negative aspects, and yet they are simply necessary
garbage to be thrown away in contempt by the entire gigantic
social structure. However, they should not blind us to the
majesty of the basic concept and its scope. During the period
when Saladin was winning his glorious victory over the
Crusaders, how do we know what the average street-dweller in
Cairo was living through? While Muhammad 'Ali was busy creating an Egyptian empire in the nineteenth century, how much
did the Egyptian peasants have to suffer? Have we ever tried
to imagine what it must have been like during the time of the
Prophet himself, when the new faith caused deep rifts
between father and son, brother and brother, and husband and
wife? Friendships were torn apart, and long-standing traditions
were replaced by new hardships. And if we keep all these
precedents in mind, should we not be willing to endure a bit of
pain and inconvenience in the process of turning our state, the
most powerful in the Middle East, into a model of a scientific,
socialist, and industrial nation? While all these notions were
buzzing inside my head, I had the sense that, by applying such
logic, I could even manage to convince myself that death itself
had its own particular requirements and benefits.

And then, all of a sudden one afternoon, the familiar, long-
lost faces reappeared in the doorway: Zaynab Diyab, Isma'il

al-Shaykh, Hilmi Hamada, and some others as well. We never saw the rest of them again. Their arrival prompted an instantaneous outburst of pure joy, and we all welcomed them back with open arms. Even Zayn al-'Abidin joined in the festivities. Qurunfula sank back into her chair, as though she were taking a nap or had just fainted. She neither spoke nor moved. Hilmi Hamada went over to her.

"I'll get my revenge on you!" she sobbed and then burst into tears.

"Where on earth have you all been?" someone asked.

"On a trip," more than one voice answered.

They all roared with laughter, and everyone seemed happy again. And yet their faces had altered. The shaved heads made them look peculiar, and the old youthful sparkle in their eyes had gone, replaced by listless expressions.

"But how did it all happen?" someone (maybe Zayn al-'Abidin) asked.

"No, no!" yelled Isma'il al-Shaykh, "please spare us that. . . ."

"Oh, come on," yelled Zaynab Diyab gleefully. "Forget about all that. We've come through it, and we're all safe and sound."

There was one name that I kept hearing, although I have no idea how it came up or who was the first person to mention it: Khalid Safwan, Khalid Safwan. So who was this Khalid Safwan? A detective? Prison warden? Several of them kept mentioning his name. I caught brief glimpses of the expressions on their faces; under the exterior veil the suffering and sense of disillusionment were almost palpable.

True enough, life at Karnak Café resumed its daily routine, and yet a good deal of the basic spirit of the place had been lost. A thick partition had now been lowered, one that turned the time they had been away into an ongoing mystery, an engrossing secret that left questions of all kinds unanswered. Beyond that, and in spite of all the lively chatter and jollity, a new atmosphere of caution pervaded the place, rather like a peculiar smell whose source you cannot trace. Every joke told had more than one meaning to it; every gesture implied more than one thing; in every innocent glance there was also a feeling of apprehension.

One day Qurunfula opened up to me. "Those young folk have been through a great deal," she said.

"Has he told you anything about it?" I asked eagerly.

"No," she replied, "he doesn't say a single word. But that in itself is enough."

Yes indeed, that in itself was enough. After all, we were all living in an era of unseen powers—spies hovering in the very air we breathed, shadows in broad daylight. I started using my imagination to reflect upon the past. Roman gladiators, courts of inquiry, reckless reprobates, criminal behavior, epics of suffering, ferocious outbursts of violence, forest clashes. I had to rescue myself from these reflections on human history, so I reminded myself that for millions of years dinosaurs had roamed the earth, but it had only taken a single hour to eradicate them all in a life-and-death struggle. All that remained now were just one or two huge skeletons. It seems that, whenever darkness envelops us, we are intoxicated by power and tempted to emulate the gods;

with that, a savage and barbaric heritage is aroused deep within us and revives the spirit of ages long since past.

At this particular moment all the information I had was filtered through the imagination. It was only years later and in very different circumstances that people finally began to open their hearts, hearts that had previously been locked tight shut. They provided me with gruesome details, all of which helped explain certain events that at the time had seemed completely inexplicable.

Zayn al-'Abidin never for a moment gave up hope, making a virtue out of patience. He kept on watching and waiting for just the right moment. Needless to say, Hilmi Hamada's return had completely ruined his plans. It may have been his fear of seeing his quest for Qurunfula end in failure that stirred an emotion buried deep inside him. In any case, it led him to cross a line and abandon his normally cautious demeanor. One day he put his suppressed feelings into words right in front of Qurunfula.

"It seems to me," he stated recklessly, "that the presence of these young people in the café may be having a very negative effect on the place's reputation."

Qurunfula shot right back at him. "So when are you planning to leave?" she asked.

He chose to ignore her remark and instead continued in a suitably homiletic tone, "I do have a worthwhile project in mind, one with a number of benefits to it." He now turned toward me, looking for support. "What do you think of the project?" he asked.

For my part I addressed a question to Qurunfula.

"Wouldn't you like to have a larger share in the national capital?"

"But it's not just the capital he's after," she replied sarcastically. "He wants the woman who owns it as well!"

"Not so," insisted Zayn al-'Abidin. "My proposal only involves the business itself. Matters of the heart rest in the hands of God Almighty."

She stopped arguing with him. It seemed as though she was totally consumed by her infatuation. Every time I watched her playing the role of the blind lover, I felt a tender sympathy for her plight. I had no doubt in my mind that that boy loved her in an adolescent kind of way; for her part she certainly knew how to attract him and keep him happy, while he was able to enjoy her affection to the full. But how long would it last? On that particular score she used to share some of her misgivings with me, but at the same time she felt able to tell me with complete confidence that he certainly wasn't a gigolo.

"He's as decent as he is intelligent. He's not the sort to sell himself."

I had no reason to doubt her word. The boy's appearance and the way he talked both tended to confirm her opinion, although once in a while his expression would turn cryptic and even violent. But speculation of this kind was essentially pointless when one was faced with the incontrovertible fact that Qurunfula was well into the autumn of her years; at this stage in her life, money and fidelity were the only things she could now offer from among the many forms of enticement she had previously had at her disposal.

One time Zayn al-'Abidin had a word in my ear. "Don't be fooled by his appearance," he said.

I immediately realized he was talking about Hilmi Hamada. "What do you know about him?" I asked.

"Look, he's either a world-class schmoozer or a complete and utter phony!" For a few moments he said nothing, then went on, "I'm pretty sure he's in love with Zaynab Diyab. Any day now he's going to grab her away from Isma'il al-Shaykh."

I was troubled by his comments; not because I thought he was lying, but rather because they tended to confirm what I had recently been noticing myself, the way Hilmi and Zaynab kept on chatting to each other in a certain way. I had frequently asked myself whether it was just a case of close friendship or something more than that.

My friendship with Qurunfula was now on a firm enough footing for me to summon up the necessary courage to ask her a crucial question. "You've had a lot of experience in matters of life and love, haven't you?

"No one can have any doubts on that score," she responded proudly.

"And yet . . . ," I whispered.

"And yet what?"

"Do you think your love affair is going to have a happy ending?"

"When you're really and truly in love," she insisted, "it's that very feeling that allows you to forget all about such things as wisdom, foresight, and honor."

And that forced me to conclude that there is never any point in discussing love affairs with their participants.

And then the young folk disappeared again. As with the first time, it all happened suddenly and with no warning whatsoever.

This time, however, none of us needed to go through tortures of doubt or ask probing questions. Nevertheless we were all scared and disillusioned.

Qurunfula staggered under the weight of this new blow. "I never in my life imagined," she said, "that I'd have to go through it all again." That said, the sheer agony of the whole thing drove her upstairs to her apartment.

Once she had left, it was easier for the rest of us to talk.

"I may be totally innocent and old," said Taha al-Gharib, "but now even I'm starting to worry about myself."

Rashad Magdi's expression was totally glum. "Listen," he said with a jeer, "the leaders of the 'Urabi Revolt in 1882 may have had some doubts about you, but not this time."

"I wonder what's behind it all?" asked Muhammad Bahgat.

"They're all dangerous young men," Zayn al-'Abidin 'Abdallah chimed in. "Why's everyone so surprised at what's happened to them?"

"But they're children of this revolution!"

"There are lots of people opposed to the goals of this revolution who claim to be a part of it," Zayn al-'Abidin replied with a laugh. "When I was a boy and was heading for the red-light district, I told people I was going to the mosque."

"May God forgive these people," said Taha al-Gharib. "They certainly know how to scare folk, don't they?"

A few days after this conversation had taken place, Qurunfula came over and took a seat beside me. She was looking utterly miserable. "Tell me what it all means," she asked anxiously.

I understood full well what she meant, but I pretended not to follow her.

"Someone around here is passing on secret information!"

"Could well be," I muttered.

"Rubbish!" she yelled. "It's completely obvious. Everyone's talking. The question is, who's passing it all on?"

I paused for a moment. "You know the place better than I," I said.

"I have no suspicions about my employees," she said. "'Arif Sulayman is indebted to me for his very life, and Imam al-Fawwal is a man of faith, so is Gum'a. . . ."

"How about those old men sitting there on the sidelines?"

With that we stared at each other for quite a while. "No!" she said. "Zayn al-'Abidin may be a wretch, but he has nothing to do with the authorities. In any case, he's so corrupt himself, he's scared to death of them."

"There are scores of people who come in here every day," I pointed out, "but we never pay the slightest attention to them."

She sighed. "Nothing in the world is safe any longer."

That said, the same grief-laden silence descended on the place again. She went back and sat on her chair, looking like a lifeless statue.

True enough, things like the ones we were experiencing were happening every day, but the effect is very different when the people to whom it is happening are considered part of the family. We began to be suspicious of everything, even the walls and tables. I was totally amazed at the state in which my homeland now found itself. In spite of all the wrong turns, it was growing in power and prestige, always expanding and getting bigger. It was making goods of all kinds, from needles to rockets, and broadcasting a wonderful new and humane trend in the life of humanity. But what was the point of all that if people were so feeble and downtrodden that they were not worth a fly, if they had no personal rights, no honor, no security, and if they were being crushed by cowardice, hypocrisy, and desolation?

Zayn al-'Abidin's nerves suddenly snapped for no apparent reason. "I'm so miserable," he yelled. "I'm unlucky. I feel wretched. God curse the day I was ever born or came to this damned café!"

Qurunfula studiously ignored him.

"What have I done wrong?" he carried on. "I love you. What's wrong with that? Why do you bad-mouth me every single day? Don't you realize that it kills me to see you looking so sad? Why? Don't spurn my love. Love is not to be spurned. It's far more exalted and lofty than that. I feel really sorry for you, squandering the rest of your precious life so pitilessly. Why do you refuse to acknowledge that my heart is the only one that really adores you?"

Now Qurunfula broke her silence. "It would appear," she said, addressing her comments to the rest of us, "that this man has no desire to respect my grief."

"Me!" retorted Zayn al-'Abidin. "I respect riffraff, hypocrites, criminals, pimps, and conmen, so how could I possibly not feel respect for the grief of the woman who has taught me the way to revere sorrow by feeling sorry for her? Excuse me, please! Grieve away! Surrender to your destiny, wallow in the mire of what is left of your life. May God be with you!"

"Perhaps it would be better," she said, "if you went somewhere else."

"I've nowhere else to go! Where am I supposed to go? Here at least I can discover a crazy illusion, one that offers an occasional glimmer of hope."

With that he started calming down and was soon back to normal. He looked very sheepish. As a way of drawing a veil over his outburst, he stood up with all the formality of a soldier, looked at Qurunfula, and apologized. After giving her a bow, he sat down again and started smoking his waterpipe.

Winter arrived, along with its biting cold and long nights. I remembered that the young folk used to meet here even during the wintertime—part of the academic year— even if it was just for an hour or so. Without them around, I thought to myself, this café is unbearable. The only people left now are those old men who have all completely forgotten about the other customers in prison; there they are, pretending to ignore the terror and politics by burying themselves in their own private worries. For them the only job left, it would seem, is sitting around and waiting for their final hour to come. Now they rue the passing of the good old days. Their only secret purpose in exchanging weird prescriptions is to postpone their appointment with death.

"'Eat, drink, and be merry,' the saying goes. That's the best slogan for life."

"Swill your mouth out with a cup of water! So much the better if you can squeeze half a lemon as well."

"An ancient philosopher is alleged to have said that he was amazed that Egyptians ever became ill when they had lemons."

"Modern medical research has confirmed that climbing stairs is good for your heart."

"Walking's good too."

"And so is sex, so they say."

"So what's bad then?"

"Politics, news of arrests and imprisonments, and having to be alive at the same time as great men."

"Yoghurt and fruit are terrific. As for honey on the comb, well, no words can possibly describe it adequately."

"And laughter. Don't forget laughter."

"A cup of chilled wine just before bed."

"Hormones are not to be sneezed at either."

"And a sleeping pill, just as a precaution against bad news."

"But reading the Qur'an, above all else. . . ."

Yes indeed, without having the young folk around, the café atmosphere becomes utterly unbearable. Even Qurunfula is not aware of quite how sad I'm feeling. She does not seem to realize that friendship is something powerful and that my own thirst is like love itself. Here I sit by myself, suffering through the pangs of boredom and loneliness as I stare at those silent, motionless chairs. All the

27

while there is a longing in my heart and a profound sorrow. How much I long to chat with the young folk who normally sit on those chairs and recharge my own batteries on the sheer enthusiasm, creativity, and hallowed suffering that they offer.

One evening, I arrived at the café to find Qurunfula beaming and happy, unusually so. I was taken by surprise and felt a wave of hope engulfing me. I rushed inside and found myself face to face with my long-lost friends. There they all were again: Zaynab, Isma'il, and Hilmi, along with two or three others. We all gave each other warm hugs, and Qurunfula's laughter gave us all a blessing. We kept exchanging expressions of endearment, without asking any of the normal wheres, hows, and whys. Even so, the name of Khalid Safwan kept coming up again, that name which in some way or other had become an indispensable symbol of our current lives.

"Just imagine," Qurunfula told me, "there was some kind of misunderstanding at the beginning of winter, but it was only at the beginning of the following summer that his true innocence emerged. But don't ask any more. It's enough for you just to imagine. . . . Never mind, there's nothing we can do about it."

"And let's assume at the same time," I suggested, "that this café is one gigantic ear!"

With that we decided to steer clear of politics as far as possible.

"If we absolutely can't avoid talking about some topic of national importance," I suggested again, "then let's do it on the assumption that Mr. Khalid Safwan is sitting right here with us."

But this time what had been lost was even more palpable than last time. They were all so thin; it looked as though they had just completed a prolonged fast. Their expressions were sad and cynical; at the corners of their mouths there lurked a suppressed anger. Once the conversation had warmed up a bit, these outward signs of hidden feelings would dissipate, leaving them with their own thoughts and ideas. However, once the veil was lifted, all that remained was a sense of languor and a retreat from society. Even the steady relationship between Zaynab and Isma'il was clearly suffering under the impact of some disease that was not immediately noticeable; and that aroused a profound sense of sorrow in me, not to mention a lot of questions. Good God, I told myself, here are the deities of hell concentrating all their attention on the very people with ideas and the will to carry them through. What is it all supposed to mean?

One time Qurunfula came over and sat beside me. She was looking pleased, but not entirely happy. By now I had realized that she only came over to sit with me when she had something she wanted to tell me.

"Let's pray to God," I said as a conversation opener, "not to let anything like it happen again."

"Yes," she replied sadly, "you should be praying to Him a lot. And while you're at it, tell Him how desperately we need some tangible sign of His mercy and justice."

"So what's new?"

"The person who's returned to my embrace is a shadow of his former self. Where's Hilmi Hamada gone?"

"His health, you mean? But they've all gone through the same thing. They'll get their health back again in a few days."

"Perhaps you don't realize what a proud and courageous young man he is. His kind usually suffers more than others." She looked me straight in the eye. "He's completely lost the ability to be happy!"

I did not understand what she meant.

"He's completely lost the ability to be happy," she repeated.

"Maybe you're being too pessimistic."

"No, I'm not," she replied. "I wouldn't feel so unhappy if it weren't called for." She let out one of her deep sighs. "Ever since I've been the owner of this café," she went on, "I've taken good care of it: floor, walls, furniture, everything is the way it is because I have made it my business to take good care of things. Now these people are torturing their own flesh and blood. Damn them!" She grabbed my arm. "Let's spit on civilization!"

For a long time I found myself wavering between my admiration for the great things that we had achieved and my utter repulsion for the use of terror and panic. I could see no way of ridding our towering edifice of these disgusting vermin.

It was Zayn al-'Abidin who one day was the first to share some other news with us. "There appear to be some dark clouds on the horizon," he said. He used to listen to the foreign news broadcasts and would often pick up rare bits of information.

We discussed the Palestinian raids and Israel's promise to take reprisals.

"At this rate," he went on, "we may well have a war this year or next."

All of us had complete confidence in our own armed forces.

"It's nothing to worry about," Taha al-Gharib commented, "unless, of course, America gets involved."

That was as far as that conversation went. During this particular period the only event to disturb the atmosphere was a passing storm provoked by Hilmi Hamada that almost ended his long-standing love affair. He developed the idea that Qurunfula was treating him with too much sympathy and that such behavior infringed on his sense of self-respect. He utterly rejected such coddling and made up his mind to leave the café. It was only when his friends grabbed hold of him that he was persuaded not to do so. Poor Qurunfula was totally stunned. She started apologizing to him, although she had no clear idea of what she had done wrong.

"It's unbearable to listen to the same refrain all the time," he said edgily and then turned angry. "I hate hearing people sobbing all the time." And, even more angrily, "I can't stand anything anymore."

Everyone saw the problem as a symptom of the general situation, and so, until things settled down, we all made a great effort to avoid saying anything that might complicate matters. Needless to say, Zayn al-'Abidin was delighted by the whole thing, but it did not do his cause any good. Hilmi Hamada's anger did not last very long, and he may even have come to regret allowing his temper to boil over. Qurunfula was deeply affected by it all, but did not utter a single word.

"That's the last thing I expected," she whispered in my ear.

"Do you think," I asked anxiously, "that he's become aware that you talk to me about him?"

She shook her head.

"Has he ever acted like that before?"

"No, this was the first time and, I hope and pray, the last."

"Maybe it would help if you stopped complaining and grieving so much."

"If only you realized," she sighed, "how utterly miserable he is."

≈

And then, right in the middle of spring, they all vanished for a third time.

On this occasion no questions were asked, and there were no violent reactions either. We just stared at each other, shook our heads, and said something or other that made no sense.

"Usual story."

"Same reasons."

"Same results."

"No point in thinking about it."

For a long time Qurunfula sat silently in her chair. Then she burst into a prolonged fit of laughter, until there were tears in her eyes. From our various seats we all stared at her in silence.

"Come on!" she said. "Laugh, laugh!" She used a small handkerchief to dry her eyes. "Why don't you all laugh?" she continued. "It's more powerful than tears; better for the health too. Laugh from the very depths of your hearts; laugh until the owners of every bar on this cheerful street can hear us." She was silent for a moment. "How are we supposed to go on feeling sad," she went on, "when these things keep happening as regularly as sunrise and sunset? They'll be back, and they'll sit here in our midst like so many ghosts. When they do, I swear I'm going to rename this place 'Ghosts' Café'."

She looked over at 'Arif Sulayman. "Pour all our honored customers a glass of wine, and let's drink to our absent friends."

The rest of the evening went by in an atmosphere of almost total depression.

In spite of everything, we put aside our own petty anxieties, all of which seemed purely personal when measured against the major events that were overwhelming our country as a whole. Rumors started to fly, and before we knew it, the Egyptian army was heading for Sinai in full force. The entire region erupted with pledges of war. None of us had any doubts about the efficiency of our armed forces, and yet . . . .

"America, that's the real enemy."

"If the army decides to launch an attack, warnings are going to come raining down on us."

"The Sixth Fleet will be moved in."

"Missiles will be launched at the Nile delta."

"Won't our very independence be in jeopardy?"

Indeed none of us had any doubts about our own armed forces. Certain civic values may have collapsed in front of our very eyes and the hands of my people may have been sullied, but we never doubted our armed forces. Needless to say, the entire notion was not without its naïve aspects, but our excuse was that we were all bewitched and determined to hope for the best. We were simply incapable, it seems, of calling into question the first ever genuine experiment in national rule, one that had brought to an end successive eras of slavery and humiliation.

So for the longest possible time we continued to cling to our zeal and enthusiasm. But then we had no choice but to wake up and endure that most vicious of hammer blows smashing its way into our heads, which were still filled with the heady intoxication of greatness.

I can never forget Taha al-Gharib's reaction, he being the eldest among us.

"Here I am close to death," he groaned, his expression a tissue of pain. "In a week or so I'll be dead. O God, O God, why did You have to delay things? Couldn't You have speeded things up a bit so that I would never have had to face this blackest of days?"

The hearts of our innocent people were seared with grief. The only hope still left in life was to attempt another strike and recover the land that had been lost. In spite of it all, I still heard people here and there who seemed to be relishing the moment. It was at that point that I began to realize that the struggle we were involved in was not just a matter of loyalty to homeland; even during the country's darkest hours, the national effort was liable to be sidetracked by another conflict involving interests and beliefs. In the days and years that followed I kept close track of this tendency, until its basic tenets and variegated manifestations were clearly visible. The June War of 1967 was a defeat for one Arab nation, but also a victory for other Arabs. It managed to rip the veil off a number of distasteful realities and usher in a wide-scale war among the Arabs themselves, not just between the Arabs and Israel.

Some weeks after the June War, our friends returned to the café; or, to be more precise, Isma'il al-Shaykh, Zaynab Diyab, and two others did. Even in the midst of so much grief on the national level, their return was the occasion for some temporary happiness. We all embraced warmly.

"Here we are, back again!" yelled Isma'il al-Shaykh, and then even louder, "They've arrested Khalid Safwan!"

"Many people have been transferred from government office straight to prison," commented Muhammad Bahgat.

Qurunfula was standing behind the table. "Where's Hilmi?" she asked.

No one answered.

"Where is he?" she asked again, angry and insistent. "Why hasn't he come with you?"

Still no one said a word. They all avoided looking at her.

"What's the matter?" she yelled. "Can't you speak or something?"

When no one said a word, she realized.

"No, no!" she screamed. She looked at Isma'il. "Isma'il, say something, anything, please. . . ."

She leaned over the table as though she had suffered a stomach rupture and stayed there for a while without saying anything. Then she raised her head. "Merciful God, have mercy . . . have mercy!"

She would have collapsed completely if 'Arif Sulayman had not caught her and taken her outside.

"They say he died under interrogation," said Isma'il after she had left.

"Meaning that he was murdered," commented Zaynab.

During those days that followed the June War, sorrow, just like joy, was soon forgotten. I offered my condolences to Qurunfula, but she did not seem to grasp the significance of what I was saying.

So this totally unforeseen tidal wave spread further and further. We all started following the news again and chewing the fat. As we suffered our painful way through the ongoing sequences of days, we placed the entire burden on our shoulders and proceeded on our way with labored, faltering steps. It was by sticking together that we continued to seek refuge from the sense of isolation and loneliness. It felt as if we had made a whole series of decisions about how to protect ourselves: against the blows of the unseen we would cling to each other; in the face of potential terrors we would share our opinions; when confronting overwhelming despair we would tell grisly sarcastic jokes; in acknowledging major mistakes we would indulge in torrid bursts of confession; faced with the dreadful burdens of responsibility we would torture ourselves; and to avoid the generally oppressive social atmosphere we would indulge ourselves in phony dreams. As hour followed hour, we found ourselves wading through a never-ending realm of darkness and on the verge of collapse, but never for a single second did we veer from our chosen course.

Among the café's clientele, the ones who best managed to withstand this pestilential onslaught were Imam al-Fawwal, the waiter, and Gum'a, the bootblack. Both of them adamantly refused to accept that the defeat was a reality; they kept on believing what the radio was telling them. They were still dreaming of Victory Day. But, as time went by, their sense of disaster began to dissipate, to be replaced by an increasing concern with matters of daily life. Gradually they came to adopt a more insouciant attitude, although deep down they both felt a lingering sorrow over what had happened.

The group of old men decided to retreat into the past.

"Never in all our long history have we been in such a sorry state."

"At least in the past, we used to have the law as a haven. That was all we needed."

"Even during the very worst periods of tyranny, there were always voices raised in opposition."

"Those glorious days in the past, days of struggle, defiance, and sacrifice! How can we ever forget them?"

They kept going back further and further in time, until eventually they settled some time in the seventh century with the caliph 'Umar ibn al-Khattab and the Prophet himself. They competed with each other to drag up the past, trying very hard to use the glories of yesteryear as a means of forgetting the present.

Zayn al-'Abidin 'Abdallah kept listening to their chatter with a mixture of interest and contempt. "There's only one country with the solution," he said, affording us the benefit of his opinion, "and that's America."

That seemed to strike a chord with 'Arif Sulayman, the wine-steward, who registered his agreement.

"Everything will have to start again from scratch," he declared with a sweeping gesture. "This period of recuperation we're going through is simply the last twitches before death finally comes."

The young folk were the only ones who neither gave themselves over to the past nor hoped for some goodwill gesture from America. Once they had all recovered from the blow of the June 1967 defeat, they all started talking, bit by bit, about a new struggle on the broadest possible scale, a conflict on a world-wide level between progressivist forces and imperialism. They said that people needed to be ready for a risky future; they talked about radical transformations in the basic internal fabric of society, and so on and so on.

Apart from large-scale issues, the one thing that drew my attention more than anything else was the obvious change in the relationship between Zaynab Diyab and Isma'il al-Shaykh. It seemed as if some unknown disease had crept into their hearts, making them act almost like complete strangers. I came to the conclusion that they had both buried their former love for each other once and for all and had decided to go their separate ways, taking their lives and sorrows with them. All of which led me to return to my former opinion, namely that Zaynab was actually in love with Hilmi Hamada. As time went by, I started to believe that more and more.

I was delighted to notice that Qurunfula seemed to be recovering her old energy. Most of the time she was quiet and kept to herself. She would listen to the things we were saying, but would stay out of the discussions. By this time she was starting to look more staid and older.

So time went by, and some faces disappeared, while others alternated between presence and absence. Up till now things have for the most part continued without much change. Most recently, things have worked out in such a way that my own relationships with some of the regulars at Karnak Café have been strengthened. From them I've learned things that I did not know before. Inner secrets involving both events and the hearts of men have now become known to me, and I have drained the glass to the very dregs.

ℒ Isma'il al-Shaykh ℒ

Yes indeed, I've learned things I did not know before. From the very first time we met I found Isma'il al-Shaykh interesting. He had a strong build, and his features were large and pronounced. I only ever saw him wearing one suit, and he wore it winter and summer long. In summer he used to take the jacket off, but in winter it would be back on, along with a sweater. He was obviously poor, but even so he still managed to win your respect. In spite of intermittent terms spent in prison, he had just recently earned his law diploma.

"I come from a very poor neighborhood," he told me. "Have you ever heard of Da'bas Alley in the Husayniya Quarter? My father works there in a liver restaurant, and my mother's a peddler who also sells sweet basil and palm leaves whenever people go to visit their family gravesite during the Eid festival. My elder brothers are a butcher's mate, a cart-driver, and a cobbler. Our home consists of a single room that looks out on a tenement courtyard. The whole building feels like one enormous family consisting of over fifty people. There's no bathroom or running water. The only toilet is in the corner of the yard, and we have to carry the water to it in jerry cans. The women all gather in the yard; on occasion men and women will congregate together. It's there that they exchange gossip and jokes, and occasionally insults and blows as well. They eat and pray."

He gave me a frown. "Basically nothing has changed in Da'bas Alley right up till today," he said, but then he corrected himself. "No, I'm wrong. Schools have started opening their doors to people like us. That's an undeniable boon. I was one of the children who went to school, but my father really hoped I would fail; he was anxious to get rid of me like my brothers by apprenticing me off to some tradesman. I thwarted him by doing well in my studies and eventually getting the Certificate of Secondary Education. That made it possible for me to enroll in law school. Once that happened, my father changed his tune and started treating me with pride and admiration. Could his son really turn into a public prosecutor, he wondered? In our part of town, there are always two well-known posts: policeman and public prosecutor. As you know, people have to deal with both types. My mother set her heart on my continuing my studies, 'even,' as she put it herself, 'if it means having to sell my own eyes.' God knows how much it must have cost her to buy me a suit that would look right for a university student. But for her it was a piece of real estate that needed to be properly looked after: repair it, refurbish, or even replace it, by all means, but never dispense with it."

He paused for a moment. "These days the place is crawling with boys and girls going to school," he went on angrily, "but their future is an ongoing problem that nations keep batting back and forth among each other."

When the 1952 Revolution happened, he had been three years old. Thus he was in every sense of the word a 'son of the revolution.' With that in mind, I could see no reason to conceal my amazement at the appalling treatment he had received. "It's been suggested," I told him, "that you must be either a Communist or a member of the Muslim Brotherhood."

"Neither," he replied. "My only allegiance is to the July 1952 Revolution. But when it comes to the situation today . . . ." He fell silent and started shaking his head, as though he did not know what to say next. "For a long time," he went on, "I've considered Egyptian history as really beginning on July 23, 1952. It's only since the June 1967 War that I've started looking back earlier than that."

He admitted to me that he believed in Egyptian socialism. For that reason his faith had remained unshaken.

"But what about your belief in socialist ideas now?" I asked.

"Many people have decided to vent their spleen against socialism as being one of the causes of our defeat. But what we need to realize is that there has never been any genuine socialism in our lives. That's why I've still not abandoned my support for the concept, even though I would dearly like to get rid of the people who have been applying it up till now. Hilmi Hamada—may he rest in peace!—was well aware of that from the very beginning."

"How come?"

"He was a Communist."

"So there were some strangers in your group then?"

"Yes, but what did we do wrong?"

He told me a great deal about Zaynab. "I have known her ever since we were both kids growing up in the alley. She lives in the same tenement building. We used to play games with each other and were beaten for doing so. Then she grew up and matured into a young woman. She developed physically; whenever she moved, she used to attract the attention of young men. Youthful passions were stirred, and I took it upon myself to defend her, drawing my courage from old stories about gangs in our quarter. When we were both in secondary school, spies and traditions kept interfering in our lives, but our love was very strong. Our true feelings for each other had flared into the open, and everyone was forced to acknowledge that we were in love. It was when we went to university that at last we found some freedom. We announced our engagement, but, since we both viewed marriage as the final sanctuary, decided to wait before getting married. And now, just look at the way such dreams all come to nothing, and everything dies. . . ."

He went on to tell me how they had found undreamed-of freedom at university. Their student days could not be subjected to the kind of authoritarian prudery that governed their movements in Da'bas Alley, where there had had to be a valid reason or excuse for every single absence or lateness. As a result of this new-found freedom, they had spent many long hours together and had got to know each other's friends. She had joined him and become one of the regular customers at Karnak Café; she had been arrested when he was. Her personality had developed in a way that he had never imagined.

44

"We found ourselves beset by the issue of sex," he went on with a laugh. "For a long time we both fumbled around, not really knowing what to do about it. We were both fully aware, of course, that we were surrounded by a variety of temptations urging us to indulge in experiments in free love that were all the rage.

"'We're in love,' I told her one day as I gave her a warm hug, 'there's no doubt about that. We're definitely going to get married. So what do you say?'

"'I promised my father I wouldn't,' she replied.

"'That's stupid,' I said. 'It doesn't mean anything. Don't you hear what people are saying?'

"'I'm not sure about it,' she replied testily, 'nor are you!'

"The result was that we both suffered a good deal over the subject."

So how far is this Isma'il a genuine revolutionary? I asked myself. He makes no attempt to hide his religious belief, so he's obviously a particular type of revolutionary. I wanted to ask him about his personal views on sexual freedom, but I was afraid he might get the impression that I wanted to pry into Zaynab's secrets. With that in mind, I decided not to take him down a path that might lead him to reveal things he preferred not to be public knowledge.

"In spite of everything people believe," he said, "true love can provide a bulwark against temptation."

There was something else he told me as well, and I can never forget it.

"In prison we felt a terrible sense of loss, and it managed to shake the entire foundation of our love for each other."

That reminded me that violent convulsions in a man's life are followed by cries for help in sexual guise that often verge on the insane. What did it all mean? I wondered. But he seemed reluctant to return to the subject, so I changed the subject.

"What about Hilmi Hamada?" I asked.

"He kept on breaking with tradition and always did it with enormous intensity."

"Was he from the same background as you?"

"No, certainly not! His father was a teacher of English, and his grandfather worked on the railroad."

"Was he really in love with Qurunfula?"

"Certainly," he replied, "I have absolutely no doubt about that. It may have been purely by chance that we initially found the café, but he insisted on going back to it. I can remember him saying, 'Let's go back to that woman's café. She's very attractive. Didn't you notice?' To tell the truth, we wanted to go back too, since we had grown fond of her as friends."

I had no doubts about Qurunfula's attractiveness either, since I had fallen under the same spell. But was all that enough to counteract the powerful impression I had that Hilmi Hamada had been in love with Zaynab? Wasn't it possible, I asked myself, that he had publicized his love for Qurunfula as a way of hiding his true feelings?

"Yes, he really loved Qurunfula. Mind you, his motives may not have been entirely flawless. What he was looking for may have been something similar to love without actually being true love itself. Even so, he was loyal to her and

46

showed her genuine affection. He never gave in to the urge to exploit her feelings, however easy that might have been. There was an idealistic side to his behavior as well. Beyond that his financial situation was fine; on that score all we need tell you is that my general education, and Zaynab's too, came about thanks to the books that we borrowed from his library."

"Perhaps he felt some pangs of sympathy for her glorious past?"

"We all used to sit there listening to her talk and pretending to believe it all," Isma'il replied with a laugh. "In fact, he didn't believe a word of it. We loved her for what she is now. Even so, he did poke fun at her claims to have modernized art and to have been the only one of her profession who behaved in a model fashion."

"With regard to both art and morals," I commented as a neutral observer, "she was certainly a model for emulation."

"It's too late to convince Hilmi of that now," he replied.

But why had Isma'il al-Shaykh been put in prison? As before, I was afraid that he would not respond to that question, but the radical change in circumstances seemed to have led him to adopt a different attitude.

"It was nighttime," he said. "I was asleep on a bench in the yard. In spring and fall I always do that so as to leave the single room for my father. I was sound asleep. Gradually I became aware of daylight impinging on my sleep like a dream. Someone was shaking me roughly. I woke up, opened my eyes, but found myself blinded by a powerful light shining right into my eyes. I sat up with a start.

"'Where's the al-Shaykh house?' a voice asked.

"'This is it,' I replied. 'What do you want? I'm his son, Isma'il.'

"'Fine,' said the voice.

"The flashlight went out, and everything went dark. After a while I could make out some figures.

"'Come with us.'

"'Who are you?'

"'Don't worry, we're police.'

"'What do you want?'

"'You just need to answer a few questions. You'll be back home before daybreak.'

"'Let me tell my father and put my suit on.'

"'There's no need for that.'

"A hand grabbed me by the shoulder, and I submitted. Wearing only my nightshirt I was frog-marched barefoot outside and thrust into a car. One of them sat on either side of me. Even though it was still pitch-dark, they put a blindfold over my eyes and tied my hands. My knees were left untied.

"'Why are you treating me like this when I've done nothing wrong?' I asked.

"'Shut up!'

"'Take me to someone in authority, and you'll see.'

"'That's exactly where you're going now.'

"With that I felt a deathly terror. I started wondering what the charge might be. I wasn't a Communist, a member of the Muslim Brotherhood, or a feudalist. I had never uttered a single word to undermine the honor of that historical period

48

which I had come to consider my own ever since I had reached the age of awareness.

"Somewhere or other, the car stopped, and I was taken out. With two men holding on to my arms, I was led blindfolded into some building. My arms were released, and I could hear the sound of footsteps retreating and the door creaking as it was shut and locked. My hands had been untied and the blindfold taken off, but I could not see a thing. I felt as though I had lost my sight. I cleared my throat, but there was no response. I expected the darkness to dissipate a little as soon as my eyes were used to it, but that did not happen. There was not a single sound. What kind of place could this be? I stretched out my arms and started feeling my way around, moving very cautiously. The floor felt cold to my bare feet. The only thing I came into contact with was the walls; there was absolutely nothing in the room, no chairs, no rug, nothing standing at all. Darkness, emptiness, despair, terror, that was it. In a dark and silent environment like that, time stops altogether; since I had no idea when they had picked me up, that was even more the case. I had no idea when the darkness was supposed to disappear or when some form of life would emerge from this all-embracing corpse of a place.

"But there is one thing that I need to tell you: when suffering pushes someone too far, he can still get the better of it. Even in moments of the direst possible agony, he can still leap up and express his concerns with a level of recklessness that can be regarded as a sign of either despair or power—both are equally valid.

49

"So I surrendered myself to the fates and decided to allow the very devil himself to come if that was indeed what destiny had determined was to be my lot, or even death if it came to that. I stopped posing myself questions for which there were no answers, but made up my mind to take the lead from the way influenza behaves, countering antibiotics by creating a whole new generations of bacteria that are resistant to medicine."

"Did you stay on your feet for a long time?" I asked.

"When the strain of it all really got to me," he said, "I squatted and then sat cross-legged on the floor. I slept as much as I could. Can you imagine? When I woke up, I remembered where I was. I realized that I had completely lost all sense of time. What time was it when I had fallen asleep? Was it daytime or night now? I felt my chin and decided to use its growth as a very inaccurate timepiece."

"Did they leave you there for long?"

"Yes."

"How about food?"

"The door used to open, and a tray would be pushed inside with some cheese on, it or else something salty with bread."

"What about the toilet?"

"At a specific time each day, the door would open again, and a giant man the size of a circus wrestler would call me outside and take me to the latrine at the end of the corridor. As I followed him, I would have to keep my eyes almost closed because the light was so bright. I had hardly closed the door behind me before he would start yelling, 'Get a move on, you son of a bitch! Do you think you can stay in there all day, you bastard?' I'll leave you to imagine how I was managing inside."

"Have you any idea how long you were there?"

"God alone knows. My beard grew so long, I couldn't tell any more."

"But they cross-examined you, for sure?"

"Oh yes," he replied with a frown. "There came the day when I found myself standing in front of Khalid Safwan."

For a moment he was silent, his eyes narrowing with the sheer emotion aroused by the memory. Inevitably I now felt myself being drawn into the intense feelings he was experiencing.

"There I stood in front of his desk, barefoot and wearing only a shoddy nightshirt. My nerves were completely shot. Behind me stood one person, or maybe more. I was not allowed to look either right or left, let alone behind me. For that reason I couldn't tell where I was and had to stare blearily straight at him. Whatever vestiges of my humanity may have been left at this point dissolved in an all-encompassing sense of terror."

For just a moment his expression was etched with suppressed anger. "In spite of everything that happened," he went on, "his image is indelibly recorded deep inside me. Of medium height, he had a large, elongated face with bushy eyebrows that pointed upwards. He had big, sunken eyes and a broad, prominent forehead. His jaw was strong, but he managed to keep his expression totally neutral. I can vividly recall all those details. Even so, I was feeling so

51

utterly desperate that I managed to create an illusion of hope for myself concerning his role.

"'Thank God!' I said. 'At last, I find myself standing before someone with authority.'

"A sharp cuff from behind cut me off, and I let out a groan of pain.

"'Only speak when you're asked a question,' he said.

"He proceeded to ask me for my name, age, and profession, all of which I answered.

"'When did you join the Muslim Brothers?' he asked.

"The question astonished me. Now I realized for the first time what it was they were accusing me of being. 'Never for a single moment have I belonged to the Muslim Brotherhood,' I replied.

"'What's the beard for then?'

"'I've grown it in prison.'

"'Are you suggesting that you haven't been well treated here?'

"'My dear sir,' I replied in a tone that was tantamount to an appeal for help, 'the treatment I have received here has been appalling and utterly unjustified.'

"'God forbid!'

"I realized at once that I had just made a dreadful mistake, but it was too late.

"'So,' he asked again, 'when did you join the Muslim Brotherhood?'

"'I never . . . ,' I started to reply but never finished the sentence. I started falling to the floor in a crumpled mass; it rushed up to greet me in a manner that seemed almost

52

magical. Khalid Safwan soon disappeared into the gloom. Later on, Hilmi Hamada told me that one of the devils standing behind me had hit me so hard that I fainted. When I came to, I was back in the same place they had taken me from—on the asphalt floor in the cell."

"What an ordeal!" I said.

"Yes, it was," he replied. "The whole thing ended suddenly and unexpectedly. What's more, it was actually in Khalid Safwan's own room."

"'We now have proof,' he told me as soon as they brought me in, 'that your name was recorded on a list because you had donated a piaster to build a mosque. You never had an actual connection with them.'

"'Isn't that exactly what I've been telling you?' I asked in a voice quivering with emotion.

"'It's an excusable error,' he replied. 'But contempt for the revolution is inexcusable.' With that he proceeded to deliver his lecture with the greatest conviction. 'We are here to protect the state that manages to keep you free of all kinds of subservience.'

"'I am one of its loyal children.'

"'Just look on the time you have spent here as a period of hospitality. Always remember how well you were treated. I trust that you'll always remember that. Just bear in mind the fact that scores of people have been laboring night and day in order to prove your innocence.'

"'I thank both God and you, sir.'"

The sheer memory of that moment led Isma'il al-Shaykh to let out a bitter laugh.

"Were other people arrested for the same reason?" I asked.

"There were in fact two members of the Muslim Brothers in our group," he replied. "They interrogated Zaynab and learned of her relationship with me, so they released her as well. It was because of us that they had arrested Hilmi. When they discovered that I was innocent, they did the same for him too."

It was all a very bitter experience for him. As a result he had come to totally distrust a government agency, namely the secret police. In spite of that, his belief in the state itself and the revolution remained rock-solid and unshaken; neither doubt nor corruption could alter his opinion on that score. As far as he was concerned, the secret police were using techniques of their own devising, but the people in authority remained in the dark.

"When I was released," Isma'il said, "I thought about complaining to the government authorities, but Hilmi Hamada used every argument he could to stop me."

"He obviously didn't believe in the very state itself, wouldn't you say?"

"Yes."

After the dreadful defeat of June 1967, Isma'il set himself to study modern Egyptian history for the first time.

"I have to tell you," he said, "that I've been constantly surprised by the power and freedom that the opposition always had and also by the role played by the Egyptian judiciary. It wasn't a period of undiluted evil. Quite the contrary, there was a whole series of intellectual trends that deserved to continue, and indeed to grow and flourish. It is the very fact that such features have been systematically overlooked that has contributed to our defeat."

Next he told me about his second period in prison.

"I was visiting Hilmi Hamada's house," he told me. "I left at around midnight, and they arrested me on the spot. With that I found myself back in the dark and empty void."

Once again he found himself forced to ponder what the accusation might be this time. He had a long time to wait before he was to find out, and once again he went through all the tortures of hell. There he was yet again facing Khalid Safwan.

"I stood there silently," he told me. "This time I could benefit from my previous experience. Even so, I was still expecting trouble from all the same directions as before.

"'You cunning little bastard,' Khalid Safwan said, looking me straight in the eye. 'Here we were, thinking you belonged to the Muslim Brothers . . . .'

"'And I turned out to be innocent,' I replied emphatically.

"'But what was lurking just below the surface was even worse!'

"'I believe in the revolution,' I said fervently. 'That's the only true fact there is. . . .'

"'Oh, everyone believes in the revolution,' he said sarcastically. 'In this very room, feudalists, Wafdists, and Communists have all avowed their belief in the revolution!'

He gave me a cruel stare. 'So when did you join the Communists?'

"A denial was immediately on my lips, but I suppressed it. In a purely reflex action I raised my shoulders as though to hide my neck, but said nothing.

"'When did you join the Communists?' he repeated.

"I felt as though my neck were becoming increasingly constricted. I had no idea what to say, so I said nothing.

"'Don't you want to confess?'

"I remained silent, using it in much the same way as I had adopted misery inside that dark prison cell.

"'Okay!' he said.

"He gestured with his hand. I heard the sound of footsteps approaching, and my body gave a shudder. All of a sudden I became aware that someone was standing right beside me; out of the corner of my eye I could make out that she was a woman. I turned toward her in amazement. All the terror I was feeling was completely obliterated by another sensation. 'Zaynab!' I yelled, unable to stop myself.

"'So you know this woman, do you?' he asked. 'It seems to matter to you what happens to her.' He looked back and forth between the two of us with those sunken eyes of his. 'Does it matter?'

"For an entire minute I felt utterly shattered.

"'You're an educated man, and I'm sure you've some imagination,' he went on. 'Can you imagine what might happen to this poor innocent girl if you refuse to talk?'

"'What is it you want, sir?' I asked in a mournful tone that was actually addressed to the world as a whole.

"'I am still asking you the same question: when did you join the Communists?'

"'I don't remember the exact date,' I replied, thereby burying any last flicker of hope, 'but I confess to being a Communist.'

"My confession was recorded on a sheet of paper, and I was taken away."

He was taken back to his cell. Contrary to his initial expectations, he was not tortured any more. Even so, he was convinced that now he was lost.

An unspecified amount of time went by, then one day a guard came along and took him to a locked door. "Perhaps you'd like to see your friend, Hilmi Hamada," he said.

He removed the cover from the peephole and ordered Isma'il to take a look inside.

"I looked inside. What I saw was so grotesque that at first I couldn't take it all in. It was just like some surrealist painting. What I could make out was that Hilmi Hamada was hanging by his feet, silent and motionless; either he had passed out or else he was dead.

"I was so shocked and disgusted that I staggered backwards. 'That is in . . . ,' I started to say but then the words stuck in my mouth as I noticed the guard staring at me.

"'What were you saying?' he asked.

"I felt utterly sick.

"'This is in—,' you said, 'in . . . what?'

"He pushed me ahead of him. 'Inhumane, is that what you meant?' he asked. 'And what about all those blood-filled dreams you all had, were they supposed to be so humane?'"

This was followed by a further interval of time during the course of which he had suffered a bad attack of influenza in the wake of a particularly cold spell of weather. While he was still recovering, he was summoned to Khalid Safwan's office again. At that particular juncture his greatest desire was to be transferred to any other prison or jail. As it turned out, Khalid Safwan spoke first.

"'You're in luck,' he said.

"I looked at him in amazement.

"'Once again you've been proved innocent.'

"All my resources of strength deserted me, and I felt an overwhelming desire to sleep.

"'Your visit to Hilmi Hamada's house was entirely innocent, wasn't it?'

"I was terrified and had no idea what to say.

"'He's confessed, but luckily for him too we've proof that he never joined any organization or party. It's the real workers we're after, not the amateurs.'

"With that my hopes of being released perked up again.

"'You're still not saying anything,' he continued, 'out of respect for the sanctity of friendship, no doubt.' For a moment he just sat there, but then he went on, 'It's that same faith in the power of friendship that makes us want to be your friends as well.'

"When was he going to order my release? I wondered.

"'Be a friend of ours,' he said. 'You told us you were devoted to the revolution. I believe you. So why don't you be one of our friends? How do you like the idea?'

"'I'm delighted, sir.'

"'We're all children of the same revolution. We're honor-bound to protect it with all due vigor, isn't that so?'

"'Of course.'

"'But there has to be a positive attitude as well. The friendship we require has to be a positive one.'

"'I've regarded myself as a friend of the revolution from the very beginning.'

"'So how would you feel if you learned that the revolution was being threatened? Would that make you happy? Would you keep your mouth shut about it?'

"'Certainly not!'

"'That's exactly what we're asking for. You'll be going to see a colleague of ours who'll tell you the proper way to do things. But I'd like to remind you that we're a force that is in complete control of things. There are no secrets from us. Friends are rewarded, and traitors are punished. That's the way it is.'"

Isma'il's face clouded over as he recalled this particular incident. If anything, he now looked even more miserable than before.

"Could you have said no?" I asked, trying to relieve his misery a bit.

"You can always find some excuse or other," he said, "but there's no point."

So that is the way he emerged from his imprisonment, an informer with a fixed salary and a tortured conscience. However hard he struggled with himself to conceptualize his new job in terms of his strong ties to the revolution, he always ended up feeling utterly appalled at what he was doing.

"When I met Zaynab again," he said, "for the first time ever I felt like some kind of stranger. Now I had a private life of my own about which she neither knew nor was supposed to know anything."

"So you kept it from her, did you?"

"Yes. I was following direct orders."

"Did you really believe they had that much authority over you?"

"Absolutely! I certainly believed it. You can add to the equation the terror factor that had totally destroyed my spirit and also my own profound sense of shame. I couldn't manage to convince myself that honor meant anything any more. I had to act in a totally reckless manner, and that was no easy matter when you consider not only my moral make-up but also my spiritual integrity. I started meandering around in never-ending torment. What made it that much worse was that, as far as I was concerned, Zaynab was a changed person too. She seemed to be overwhelmed by a profound sense of grief; the way she kept behaving provided no clue as to how she was going to get out of it. That made me feel even more of a stranger to her."

"But that was all to be expected, wasn't it?" I commented. "Things would have improved eventually."

"But I never caught even a glimpse of the Zaynab I had once known. She had always been so happy and lively; I thought nothing could ever dampen her spirit. But something had. I tried offering her encouragement, but one day she stunned me by saying that I was the one who needed encouraging!"

The week after Isma'il had been released, something absolutely incredible had happened. They had left the college grounds and were walking together.

"Where are you going now?" she asked.

"To the Karnak Café for an hour or so, then I'll go home."

"I'd like to walk alone with you for a while," she said, almost as though she were talking to herself.

He imagined that she had a secret she wanted to share with him. "Let's go to the zoo, then," he suggested.

"I want it to be somewhere safe."

Hilmi Hamada solved the problem for them both by inviting them up to Qurunfula's apartment (which was his as well). He left the two of them alone.

"Qurunfula will get the impression we're up to something," he said in a tone of innocent concern.

"Let her say what she likes!" replied Zaynab disdainfully.

He was not quite sure what to do. He took her hand in his, but she grabbed his and raised it to her neck. Their lips came together in a long kiss, and then she gave herself to him.

"The whole thing was a complete surprise," he confided to me. "I was thrilled, of course, but at the same time I couldn't help worrying. A number of unfocused questions formed a cluster inside my head. I almost asked her why she had decided to do it now, but didn't."

For a moment we just looked at each other.

"Maybe things had stirred her up?"

"Could be."

"Afterwards I regretted what I'd done. I blamed myself for taking advantage of a moment of weakness when she herself was obviously in a state of collapse as well."

"Did it happen again?"

"No."

"Neither of you thought of trying?"

"No. On the surface our ties remained strong, but something inside, in the very depths of our souls, had started to come apart."

"What a peculiar situation!"

"It felt like a lingering death. From my side, there are things that can explain it. But where she's concerned, it's a total mystery to me."

"I noticed a change in your relationship while we were at the Karnak Café, but I thought it was just something temporary that would blow over."

"I asked her what she had had to go through during her short time in prison, but she assured me it had all been short and trivial. From this point on, our beliefs in the revolution were contaminated by a deep-seated anger. We were much more willing to listen to criticism. The enthusiasm was gone; the spark was no longer there. Sure enough, the basic framework was still in place, but what we kept saying was that the style had to be changed; corruption had to be eradicated, and all those sadistic bodyguards had to go. Our glorious revolution had turned into a siege."

One evening they had discussed the subject again with Hilmi Hamada.

"I'm surprised you can still believe in the revolution!" Hilmi had said.

"Just because the body has bowels," Isma'il had replied, "doesn't diminish the nobility of the human mind."

"Aha," commented Hilmi sarcastically, "now I can see that, like everyone else, you resort to similes and metaphors whenever your arguments are weak!"

He had looked at them both. "It's time for us to do something," he went on.

He showed them a secret pamphlet that he and some of his colleagues were circulating.

"I was absolutely astonished at his frankness," Isma'il told me. "Or, more accurately, I was stunned. I dearly wished I had never heard him say it. I remembered my secret assignment that required me to report him immediately. The very thought of it made my entire universe start to shake. The reality of the deep abyss into which I was falling now became all too apparent to me.

"By now the two of us had been talking for well over an hour; Hilmi was doing the talking while I sat there or made a few terse comments. I was completely at a loss and at the same time felt utterly disconsolate.

"'Stop those activities of yours,' I told him, 'and tear up that pamphlet!'

"'What a joker you are!' he scoffed. 'This one isn't the first, and it certainly won't be the last.'

"We left his house at about ten and walked in silence. By now the time we were spending alone together was agonizing and difficult for both of us. We parted company. She needed to go back to the tenement building, while I felt like going to the Karnak Café. I wandered around the

63

streets, unable to make the fateful decision. All the time I was feeling scared, scared for me and for Zaynab as well. In the end I made no decision, but returned to the tenement building at about midnight. I threw myself down on the bench in the courtyard without even taking my clothes off. I told myself that I faced a choice: either make the decision or go out of my mind. Even then I couldn't make up my mind. I postponed things till the morning, but I didn't get any sleep at all. I'd hardly fallen asleep when they came for me."

"The security police, you mean?"

"Yes."

"That very same night?"

"Yes, the same night."

"But that's staggering, unbelievable!"

"It's magic. The only explanation I have is that they must have been watching us both and listening in from a distance."

"But, in any case, you had decided not to report your friend," I said, trying as best I could to give him a bit of consolation.

"I can't even claim that much," he replied. "After all, I had decided not to decide."

And that is how his third prison term came about. Before dawn had even broken he found himself facing Khalid Safwan again.

"You've betrayed our trust in you," said Khalid Safwan. "You failed the very first test."

Isma'il said nothing.

"Very well," he went on. "We never force anyone to be friends with us."

He was given a hundred lashes and then thrown into the cell again, that eternal darkness.

Isma'il then proceeded to tell me about Hilmi Hamada's final battle. They said he died in the interrogation room. He had both commitment and guts. The answers he gave them stunned them. They started hitting him and in a rage he tried to retaliate. A guard pummeled him with blows until he fainted. It then emerged that he was already dead.

"I languished in that awful dark cell," he said. "I've no idea how long it went on, but I just seemed to fade into the darkness."

One day he was summoned again. He assumed that he would be seeing Khalid Safwan, but this time there was a new face. He was informed that he would be released.

"I'd found out everything that had happened even before I left the building." He paused for a moment. "From beginning to end," he went on, "I heard every single detail about the flood."

"The June War, you mean?"

"That's right. May, June, even the fact that Khalid Safwan had been arrested."

"What a time that must have been."

"Just imagine, if you can, how it felt to me."

"I think I can."

"Our entire world had gone through the trauma of the June War; now it was emerging from the initial daze of defeat. I found the entire social arena abuzz with phantoms, tales, stories, rumors, and jokes. The general consensus was that we had been living through the biggest lie in our entire lives."

"Do you agree with that?"

"Yes, I do, and with all the vigor used in the torture that had tried to tear me limb from limb. My beliefs in everything were completely shattered. I had the feeling that I'd lost everything."

"Fair enough. By now though you've gone beyond that phase, haven't you?"

"To a certain extent, yes. At least I can now raise some enthusiasm for the revolution's heritage."

"And how were things for Zaynab?"

"The same as for me. At first she had very little to say, then she clammed up for good. I can still vividly recall our first meeting after I was released. We embraced each other mechanically, and I told her bitterly that we would have to get to know each other all over again. We were both faced with an entirely new world and had to deal with it. She told me that, in such a scenario, she would be presenting herself to me as someone with no name or identity. I told her that I could now understand the full meaning of the phrase 'in the eye of the storm,' to which she replied that it would be much better for us if we acknowledged our own stupidity and learned how to deal with it, since it was the only thing we had left. When I told her that Hilmi Hamada had died in prison, she went very pale and spent a long time buried in her own thoughts. She told me that we were the ones who had killed him; not only him, but thousands like him. Although I didn't really believe what I was saying, I replied

66

that we were really the victims. After all, stupid people could be considered victims too, couldn't they? Her reply came in an angrily sarcastic tone, to the effect that it all depended on quite how stupid people had actually been.

"And then, as you well know, everyone fell into the vortex. We were all assailed by various plans: plans for war, plans for peace. In such a stormy sea all solutions seemed like a far-off shore. But then there came that single ray of hope in the emergence of the fedayeen."

"So you believe in them do you?"

"I'm in touch with them, yes. Actually I'm seriously thinking of joining them. Their importance doesn't lie simply in the extraordinary things they're doing; equally significant are the unique qualities they possess, as clearly shown by these events. They're telling us that the Arabs are not the kind of people others think they are, nor indeed the kind of people they themselves think they are. If the Arabs really wanted it, they could perform wonders of courage. That's what the fedayeen believe."

"But does Zaynab agree with you?"

For a long time he said nothing. "Don't you realize," he eventually went on, "that there's nothing between us any more? All we have left are memories of an old friendship."

Needless to say, I was anticipating such a response, or something like it, since it corroborated all my own observations and deductions. Even so, I was astonished to hear him describe it that way. "Did it happen suddenly?" I asked.

"No, it didn't," he replied. "But it's difficult to hide a corpse's stench, even when you've buried it. There came the point, especially after we'd both graduated, when we had to think about getting married. I discussed it with her, keeping all my suppressed and bitter feelings to myself. For her part, she neither refused nor consented; better put, she wasn't enthusiastic. I couldn't fathom the reason why, but I had to accept the situation the way it was. After that, we only broached the topic on rare occasions and no longer felt the need to spend all our time together as we'd done in the past. We used to sit in Karnak Café acting like colleagues, not lovers. I can clearly remember that signs of this situation began to show themselves after our second term in prison, but they began to assume major proportions after the third. It was then that our personal relationship started to flag. It kept gradually falling apart until it died completely."

"So it's over then?"

"I don't think so. . . ."

"Really?"

"We're both sick. At least I am, and I know the reason why. She's sick too. One day our love may be revived; otherwise it'll die for good. At any rate, we're still waiting, and that doesn't bother either of us."

So they're both waiting. But then, who isn't?

❧ Zaynab Diyab ❧

Zaynab was both vivacious and pleasant, a combination that drew me to her from the first. She had a wonderful wine-dark complexion, and her figure had bloomed sweetly and with a certain abandon; she looked both svelte and trim. She seemed well aware that I admired her fascinating personality; in fact that was what allowed us to get to know each other well and eventually to develop a really strong sense of friendship.

She had grown up in the same surroundings as Isma'il; in the very same building, in fact.

Her father was a butcher, and her mother started out as a washerwoman before becoming a broker after a good deal of effort. She had a brother, who worked as a plumber, and two married sisters. As a result of her mother's second job the family could afford some of life's necessities; for Zaynab she was able to provide the bare minimum of clothing she needed. They were not prepared for the way Zaynab excelled in her school work, and it caused both surprise and problems. They could see no harm in allowing her to continue playing this game with education until some nice young man came along. That was why her mother did not welcome Isma'il al-Shaykh at first. She thought he was a layabout and a distinct roadblock to the future progress of any pretty young girl. Truth to tell, Zaynab's mother was the real power in the household. Her father worked hard all day for a few piasters and then proceeded to squander it all at the beer parlor. The standard result was a fierce family quarrel. The amazing thing was that her dissolute father was actually very good-looking; his austere face may have had hair sprouting from it and a mass of wrinkles to go with it, but his features were very handsome. It was from him that Zaynab had inherited her looks. Meanwhile, her virago of a mother was just as tough as any man.

The long-anticipated crisis had finally arrived when Zaynab was in secondary school. A chicken seller who was considered to be wealthy in the terms of this poor quarter came to ask for her hand. He was forty years old and a widower with three daughters. Zaynab's mother welcomed the idea of him taking her away from the tenement courtyard and giving her a happy life of her own. However, Zaynab turned him down, and that made her mother very angry. It was Isma'il and his family who had borne the brunt of that anger.

"You'll be sorry!" she yelled at her daughter. "It'll be too late, and then you'll regret it."

Even then the matter did not blow over quietly. The merchant spread a rumor that there was something going on between Zaynab and Isma'il. This also raised a storm inside the courtyard, but Zaynab's will was still strong enough to triumph. It also affected the way she behaved. In order to confront these unjust accusations head on, she decided to act in a very conservative fashion. If certain people decided to accuse her of being reactionary, then so be it; she did not care. Nor did her increasingly broad education change her demeanor in any way.

"We represent a conservatism that is deliberately dressed in the guise of progressivism," she said. "That's why, within the framework of the revolution, I've found things that to me seem both comforting and reassuring."

She loved Isma'il very much and fully understood the way he thought as well. She believed that they shared the same set of attitudes. Even though he might pretend to say things that he didn't really believe in his heart of hearts, she realized that he would never forgive her if she were to look down on him in any way.

"At the time," she told me, "old Hasaballah, the chicken seller, was eager to get me at any price. When I turned him down, he wasn't put off. He used an old woman who worked with him to get to me again. But I certainly taught her a lesson."

"You mean, he wanted to have you out of wedlock?"

"That's right. And he was prepared to pay a high price for it too!"

She was saying all this in a listless tone that seemed strangely inappropriate to the situation. At the time I had no idea what lay behind it.

"Zayn al-'Abidin 'Abdallah tried the same game later on," she said.

"Never!" I exclaimed in surprise.

"Oh yes, he did," she replied emphatically.

"But he was crazy about Qurunfula!"

She shrugged her shoulders.

"Maybe he was just pretending to be in love with her," I suggested. "He wanted to hide the fact that he was really after her money."

"No," she replied. "He was genuinely in love with her; he still is. He just needed a bit of diversion for consolation's sake. Maybe the old rogue thought I was one of those girls who fools around."

"When did he let you know what he was after?"

"Many times, but I'm referring to the first time, immediately after our first spell in prison."

"In spite of his stubbornness I believe that he's given up hope about Qurunfula."

"Why should he give up hope? He's simply sitting around waiting for the time when he'll get his dues."

She decided to put an end to this chatter about affairs of the heart. "There were many others as well," she said.

"Was Hilmi Hamada—God rest his soul—one of them?" I asked with a great deal of hidden concern.

"Certainly not!" she replied in amazement.

"I must tell you in all candor that I'd thought there was something between the two of you."

"We were close friends," she replied sadly. "But Isma'il's the only man I've ever loved."

"Are you still in love?" I asked.

She ignored my question.

The story of her attitude toward the revolution was exactly the same as Isma'il's. "They arrested me because of my connection with Isma'il," she said, talking about her first arrest. "There was not even the slightest suspicion of a case against me, and I told them I'd never been a member of the Brotherhood. I was only held for a couple of days, then released unharmed." She gave me a sad smile. "The real trouble was at home. My mother told me that those were precisely the kind of difficulties I should have expected to find myself in because of my being with Isma'il. It so happened that my own arrest came one week after my father had been taken in; he'd been accused of rowdiness and assaulting a police officer."

"In such circumstances," I commented admiringly, "the way you have managed to move ahead is remarkable."

"I asked Khalid Safwan why they were badgering us like this. We were all children of the revolution, I told him; we owed it everything. How could they accuse us of being opposed to it? His sarcastic response was to the effect that the very same excuse was being used by ninety-nine percent of the people who were genuinely opposed to the revolution."

She talked to me about her former belief in the revolution and about the fact that their imprisonment had done nothing to alter or take away their core belief in its values. "However, whereas we had previously thought that we had all the power in the world, that feeling had been severely jolted by the time we'd emerged from prison. We'd lost much of our courage and along with it our self-confidence and belief in the workings of time. We had now discovered the existence of a terrifying force operating completely outside the dictates of law and human values."

Zaynab told me that she had discussed with Isma'il the agonies she had gone through when he had suddenly disappeared. "Wouldn't it be a good idea," she had suggested, "for us to keep to ourselves for a while and avoid meeting friends and other groups?"

"It was my fault that they were all arrested," he had replied sarcastically, "not vice versa!"

I did my best to console her. "This is the kind of thing humanity has to go through," I said. "It's part of the price of all great revolutions."

She let out a sigh. "When will life be really pleasant, I wonder? Will we ever be finally rid of these dreadful miseries?"

She now started talking about her second prison term. I immediately realized that I was about to hear a tale with some truly awful memories attached to it.

"This time we were accused of being Communists," she said and then went on nervously, "it's a period in my life that I'll never forget."

She told me how she'd been taken to see Khalid Safwan again.

"So here we are again!" he had said sarcastically. "Our friendship is becoming well established!"

"Why have I been arrested?" she asked. "For my part I've no idea."

"Ah, but I do."

"Then what's the reason, sir?"

"It all goes back to those two distinguished gentlemen, Marx and Lenin." He stared at her angrily. "Now answer my questions, but make sure you don't use that silly nonsense again. You know: 'Why do you keep on badgering me?' 'We're all children of the revolution,' and so on. Understand?"

"We're not Communists," she replied, totally despairing of ever being able to persuade him.

"That's a shame!" he uttered cryptically.

She told me that she had been thrown into a cell and subjected to the most humiliating forms of torture, the pain of which only a woman could possibly appreciate fully.

"I had to live, sleep, eat, and carry out my bodily functions all in one place! Can you imagine?"

"No," I responded sadly.

"At any moment," she went on, "I might look up and see the guard leering at me through the peephole in the door. Can you appreciate what that meant?"

"Unfortunately I can."

"One day I was summoned to Khalid Safwan's office while Isma'il was being interrogated. When I saw how humiliated and hopeless he looked, tears welled up in my eyes. From the very bottom of my heart I poured curses on the world. But I was only there long enough for him to hear the threat of my being tortured. I was taken back to my filthy cell where I cried for a long time. Day after day the torture continued."

She continued her tale by telling me about another occasion when she had been summoned to Khalid Safwan's office.

"'I hope you approve of our accommodations,' he said.

"'Oh yes, sir,' I replied bravely. 'Thank you very much.'

"'Our friend's confessed to being a Communist,' he went on.

"'Only when you threatened him!' I yelled.

"'But it's the truth, however the information was obtained.'

"'Absolutely not, sir. The entire thing's atrocious.'

"'Oh no, my dear,' he replied cryptically. 'It's marvelous.'

"'How so, marvelous?'

"'We'll see,' he replied. With that he gave a specific hand-gesture.

"I heard the sound of footsteps approaching. They came closer and closer till they seemed almost to envelop me. What can I say?"

She had to stop for a moment, and the muscles in her jaw visibly tightened. Now I readied myself to hear something even worse than what had already happened.

"We can stop if you like," I suggested.

"No," she said. "It makes for good listening." She looked me straight in the eye. "At this point he decided to put on a titillating and exciting spectacle for himself, something utterly beyond the bounds of normalcy and decency."

"My dear Zaynab," I asked, my heart pounding, "what on earth do you mean?"

"You've got it right."

"No!"

"Down to the last detail."

"Right in front of him?"

"That's it, right in front of him!"

There now followed a prolonged silence, like a prolonged, mute sob.

"What kind of man can he be?" I eventually managed to mutter, referring to Khalid Safwan.

"There's nothing odd about the way he looks," Zaynab said. "For that matter he could just as well be a professor or a man of religion."

"The entire matter needs further study," I said, feeling utterly nonplussed.

"Study?" she yelled. "Did you say 'study'? Do you seriously propose to initiate a research program involving my personal honor?"

I felt so ashamed, I didn't say another word.

~

"A few weeks later I was summoned to Khalid Safwan's office again. He looked as calm as usual, even more so perhaps. It was just as though nothing had ever happened.

"'You've been proved innocent,' he said tersely.

"For a long time I simply looked straight at him. For his part, he gave me a fixed, lackadaisical stare.

"'Were you watching?' I screamed at him.

"'I simply see what there is to be seen,' he replied quietly.

"'But now I've lost everything,' I shouted angrily.

"'Oh no! Everything can be put right. We can see to that.'

"'I don't believe,' I yelled madly, 'that the revolution would be happy to hear what went on in this room!'

"'We're here to protect the revolution, and that's much more important that the few isolated mistakes we may happen to make. We always make sure to put right whatever needs to be put right. You'll be leaving here now with a brand new boon—our friendship.'

"With that I burst into tears, a prolonged fit of nervous weeping that I was totally unable to stop. He waited silently until I'd finished.

"'You're going to see one of my assistants now,' he said. 'He's going to make you an offer beyond price.' For a few moments, he said nothing, then he went on, 'I would strongly advise you not to turn it down. It's the chance of a lifetime.'"

So Zaynab had become an informer as well. She was offered special privileges, and it was decided that Isma'il was to be the pawn in the whole thing. It was made very clear to her that she had to maintain total silence; she was told that the people she was working for had absolute control of everything.

"When I went home," Zaynab told me, "and had some time to myself, I was utterly horrified by what I'd lost, something for which there could be no compensation. For the first time in my entire life I really despised myself."

"But . . . ," I began trying to console her.

"No, don't try to defend me," she interrupted. "Defending something that is despicable places you in the same category." She continued angrily, "I kept telling myself that I'd become a spy and a prostitute. That was the state I was in when I met Isma'il again."

"I assume you kept your secret to yourself."

"Yes."

"You were wrong to do that, my dear!"

"My secret job was far too dangerous to reveal to anyone else."

"I'm talking about the other matter."

"I was too afraid and ashamed to tell him about it. I was keeping my hopes up as well. I told myself that, if I had things put right by surgery, then I might be able to think about a happy life in the future."

"But that hasn't happened so far, has it?"

"Small chance!"

"Maybe I can do something for you," I offered hopefully.

"Forget it," she replied sarcastically. "Just wait till I've finished my story. I may have made a mistake, but in any case I proceeded to take the only course open to me, torturing my own self and submitting to the very worst punishments I could possibly imagine. By taking such action I was relying on an unusual kind of logic. I'm a daughter of the revolution, I convinced myself. In spite of everything that's happened, I refuse to disavow everything it stands for. Therefore I am still responsible for its welfare and must fulfill that obligation. As such, I am implicitly to blame for the things that have happened to me. On that basis I decided to stop pretending to live an honorable life and instead to behave like a dishonorable woman."

"You did yourself a grievous wrong."

"I could tolerate everything about it except the idea that Isma'il might come to despise me. At the same time I

79

didn't want to betray him. While I was going through all this, I couldn't even think straight and went completely astray." She shook her head sadly. "A number of things happened which made it impossible for me to put things right again or to return to the straight and narrow. It was at precisely that point that old Hasaballah, the chicken seller, saw me again."

I stared at her in alarm.

"This time he found the path wide open."

"No!"

"Why not? I told myself that this was the way to lead a debauched life. You couldn't do that without there being a price to pay."

"I don't believe you!"

"I took the money."

With that I felt a sense of revulsion toward the entire world.

"And Zayn al-'Abidin 'Abdallah as well!" she continued, giving me a sarcastic and defiant stare.

I didn't say a word.

"He used Imam al-Fawwal and Gum'a, the bootblack, as go-betweens," she added.

"But I always thought they were both decent, loyal people," I blurted out in amazement.

"So they were," she replied sadly. "But just like me, they were both devastated. What's happened to everyone? We seem to have turned into a nation of deviants. All the costs in terms of life—the defeat and anxiety—they have managed to demolish our sense of values. The two of them kept hearing about corruption all over the place, so what was to stop them having a turn too? I can tell you that both of them are acting as pimps as we speak and without the slightest sense of shame."

"But Zaynab," I asked, "should we despair about everything?" After a moment's pause I proceeded to answer my own question, "No! This particular phase we're going through is just like the plague, but afterwards life will be renewed once again."

Zaynab paid no attention to what I was saying. "I decided to tell Isma'il everything," she said.

"But you said you wouldn't," I said in amazement.

"I decided to do it in a very original way, so I just gave myself to him."

"I must confess that at this point I can't work out what kind of relationship there is between you and Isma'il."

"After the storm that we've been through, there's no point in trying to find some fixed logical process to apply."

"But do you still love Isma'il?"

"I've never been in love with anyone else."

"What about now?"

"All I can feel now is death, not love."

"But Zaynab, you're a young girl right at the beginning of her life. Everything will change."

"Will it be for better or worse, do you think?"

"It can't possibly get any worse than it is now. So change must be for the better."

"Let's go back to my story. The only consolation I was getting out of what I was doing was that I could feel the pain involved in the self-punishment. But then I did something that can never be expiated, no matter what the price."

"Really?"

"Yes. Are you starting to feel disgusted with me?"

"No, Zaynab," I replied. "I'm actually feeling very sorry for you."

"One evening Isma'il and I went to Hilmi Hamada's home. We found he was planning revolution. He confided in us that he was distributing secret pamphlets. . . ."

The sheer force of the memory was so great that she had to stop talking for a while. For my part, I welcomed this break that had arrived like some kind of truce-period in the midst of a prolonged saga of torture.

"His frank admission came as a total surprise to me. I dearly wished that I'd not gone to his home."

"I can well understand your feelings."

"I immediately thought of the force that was in control of everything. I was overwhelmed by panic and started worrying about Isma'il."

Aha! So there was Isma'il assuming they had used special methods to find out that he had failed to communicate with them, when all the time it had never even occurred to him that it was Zaynab who had given Hilmi away. So she was the one who had revealed his secret, assuming that by so doing she would be sparing him even greater agonies.

We stared sadly at each other.

"So I'm the one who killed Hilmi Hamada," she said.

"No, you're not," I replied. "He was killed by whoever it was made the decision to torture all of you."

"I'm the one who killed him. And they arrested Isma'il even so. Why? I don't understand. This time he spent even longer in prison than the two previous times. When he came out, he was even more crushed than before. Why? I don't know. In my report I'd put down that he'd argued with his friend and advised him to abandon the project. But any appeal to logic in these circumstances is obviously futile."

"At the time you were out of prison, weren't you?"

"Oh yes. I was free to enjoy my liberty to the full, along with all the suffering and loneliness that went with it. And then, along came the precursors of war, bringing their threats to our very existence. Like everyone else, I had a limitless trust in our armed forces. Everything would go on and on, I told myself, both good and bad. But then came the disaster and . . . ."

She fell silent; her expression was one of total dismay.

"There's no need to explain," I assured her. "We all went through it. But did you support the demonstrations on the ninth and tenth of June?"

"Yes, I certainly did, and to the maximum extent possible."

"So your basic faith has not been shaken then?"

"Quite the contrary, it has been completely uprooted from its foundations. I've come to believe that it's a castle built on sand."

"I have to tell you that I don't understand your attitude."

"It's all very simple. All of a sudden, I found I could no longer tolerate having to shoulder responsibility. After relying on a laissez-faire attitude for so long, I found that I was actually afraid of genuine freedom. How about you? Were you for or against the demonstrators at the time?"

"I was with them all the way, clinging desperately to a last spark of national pride."

"When I heard that Isma'il was going to be set free," she went on angrily, "I told myself that I had the defeat to thank for letting me see him again."

As I thought about what she had just said, the entire idea made me feel utterly sad and miserable.

Then she told me about her first meeting with Isma'il after his release, and the confused babble of their conversation.

"You know, when we first graduated and got jobs, we talked all the time about getting married, that being a requirement enjoined by traditional notions of modesty. We talked about it over and over again. It's not so strange for me to have changed and abandoned the dreams of the past, but what has caused such a change in Isma'il? What really happened inside that prison, I wonder?"

So, at this point, each one of them acknowledges that they have changed, but keeps asking himself or herself about the other one. They're both convinced that they can't live a normal life now; on that score I tend to agree with them— at least, with regard to this wretched period we're now living through. All of us need time so we can bandage our wounds and purify the collective national soul. In fact, the process may even involve a recovery of self-confidence and self-respect as well. But by the very nature of things matters like that could not be discussed in this particular context.

"If humanity simply gives up or waits," I commented, using generalities as a smoke screen, "it will never change— for the better, I mean."

"It's so easy to philosophize, isn't it!" she retorted angrily.

"Maybe so," I said, "but these days Isma'il seems to be edging toward the fedayeen."

"I know."

"And what about you?" I asked after another pause. "What are your thoughts?"

She said nothing for a while. "Before I give you a reply," she said, "I must first correct something that I said about Imam al-Fawwal and Gum'a. Actually they knew nothing about the details of the arrangement they made between Zayn al-'Abidin 'Abdallah and me after our second period in prison; they had no idea what was going on."

"Do you mean they're innocent of what you accused them of doing?"

"No, I don't. But they've only given in to temptation recently, not before. Things are still really confused in my own mind, and I want you to keep in mind that I'm telling you my own story from memory. I can't guarantee that all the details are accurate."

I nodded my head sadly. "What are your thoughts now?" I repeated.

"Do you really want to know?"

"I assume you're not still . . . ." I stopped in spite of myself.

"Being a prostitute, you mean?" she said, completing my sentence for me.

I said nothing.

"Thank you for thinking so well of me," she said.

Again I did not comment.

"At the moment," she said, "I'm living a very puritan existence."

"Really?" I asked happily.

"Certainly."

"And how did that come about?"

"Quickly, through a counter-revolution, but also because I still feel a sense of utter revulsion."

"Where, oh where have those former days of innocence and enthusiasm gone?" I asked affectionately.

Khalid Safwan

These days there's only one topic of conversation at Karnak Café. It dominates all other subjects, day after day, week after week, month after month, year after year. We talk about nothing else, and by that I mean all of us: Muhammad Bahgat, Rashad Magdi, Taha al-Gharib, Zayn al-'Abidin 'Abdallah, Isma'il al-Shaykh, Zaynab Diyab, 'Arif Sulayman, Imam al-Fawwal, Gum'a, and some new folk who represent the ever renewing cycle of generations. Qurunfula has now stopped wearing her mourning garb. She sits there, watching and listening, but never saying anything.

Often we find ourselves getting bored with the whole thing, at which point someone will suggest changing the topic before we all go absolutely mad. All of us enthusiastically support the idea and start on another subject, but discussion is usually uninspired and starts to flag. It's not too long before it's on its last legs, at which point we go back to our enduring topic. We're flogging it to death, and it's doing exactly the same thing to us, but there's no letup and no end in sight.

"War, that's the only way."

"No, the fedayeen, they're the way. And we must concentrate on defense."

"The only feasible solution is one imposed by the Great Powers as a group."

"Any negotiation implies surrender."

"But there has to be negotiation. All nations negotiate with each other. Even America, China, Russia, Pakistan, and India do just that!"

"In this instance, the idea of a 'peace settlement' means that Israel will gain complete control of the region and swallow it up in one simple gulp."

"But how come we're so afraid of a settlement? Did the English and French swallow us up?"

"If the future reveals Israel to be a state with good intentions, then we can live with it. If on the other hand it turns out to be exactly the opposite, then we'll have to get rid of it, just as we did the Crusaders many, many years ago."

"The future belongs to us. Just consider our numbers and our wealth."

"It's a question of culture and science."

"Okay then, let's go to war. That's the only solution. . . ."

"Russia isn't providing us with the weapons we need."

"No peace, no war—a stalemate. That's all that's left."

"For us, that means a process of nonstop attrition."

"No, as far as we're concerned the real struggle will take place on the cultural plane. For us peace is more risky than war."

"We should disband the army and start building ourselves up again from scratch."

"We should announce our neutrality and demand that other nations respect it."

"But what about the fedayeen? You're all ignoring the one effective force in the entire situation!"

"We've been defeated, and now we have to pay the price. We should leave the rest of it for the future."

"The Arabs' worst enemy is themselves."

"Their rulers, you mean."

"The entire government system, more like it."

"Everything depends on the Arabs being able to work as a unified entity."

"On the fifth of June 1967 at least half the Arabs won."

"Start on the inside, that's what we have to do."

"Fine! Religion then. Religion's everything."

"No! Communism's the answer."

"No! Democracy is what we need."

"Responsibility should be taken away from the Arabs altogether."

"Freedom . . . freedom!"

"Socialism."

"Let's call it democratic socialism."

"Let's start off with war. We'll have time for reforms later."

"No, the reforms have to come first, then solutions can be worked out some time in the future."

"No, the two must go hand in hand."

And so on and so on, ad infinitum.

One evening a stranger came into the café, leaning on the arm of a young man. He took a seat by the entrance.

"I'll wait for you here," he instructed the young man in an imperious tone. "You go and get the medicine. Get a move on!"

He stayed seated where he was while the young man went away. He was of medium height, with a large, elongated face, wide, bushy eyebrows, and a pronounced forehead. His eyes were wide and sunken in their sockets. He looked very pale, as though he were either sick or convalescing.

Immediately Isma'il was whispering in my ear. "See that man over there by the entrance?" he asked. "Take a good long look at him."

The newcomer had, needless to say, already attracted my attention. "What about him?" I asked.

"That's Khalid Safwan!" Isma'il replied in a trembling voice.

I was stunned. "Khalid Safwan?" I muttered back.

"The very same and in person."

"Has he been released then?"

"He's served his three-year sentence, but all his money's been sequestered."

My amazement and curiosity both got the better of me, and I started taking sneaking looks in his direction. I felt like cutting him up into pieces so I could finally discover which part of his personality was either missing or present in superabundance.

From one person to another the news gradually made its way around the café. A profound silence descended on the entire place. Everyone was staring at him. For a while he managed to ignore us all, but it did not take long for him to realize that everyone was staring at him. Once he became aware of us, it was as if he were waking up from a long sleep. Slowly and cautiously he began to look around and stare at us with those sunken eyes of his. He certainly recognized some of the faces in the café very well, Isma'il and Zaynab, for instance. He was particularly interested in Qurunfula. He stretched his legs out, and his lips formed themselves into something which might well have been a smile. Yes indeed, there it was—a smile. I had been afraid that he would panic, but no; he showed absolutely no sign of fear whatsoever. Instead what we all heard was a small voice say "Hello!"

He stared at the faces he knew so well. "Perhaps the two broken fragments will come together again," he said. He closed his eyes for a moment. "My, my," he went on as though talking to himself, "the world's certainly changed. I know this café, and now here we all are, sitting together in a single place accompanied by the direst of memories."

It was Qurunfula who responded, even though we had not heard a word out of her for ages. "Yes indeed," she said, "the direst of memories."

"These days," he told her, "you don't own exclusive rights to sorrow." His voice changed as he went on, "We're all of us simultaneously criminals and victims."

"No," she replied, "the criminal's one kind of person, and the victim's entirely different."

"We're all of us both criminals and victims," he repeated. "Anyone who can't understand that is incapable of understanding anything."

At this point the young man came back and handed him the bag of medicines. He pointed to one of the medicines on the prescription. "This one's not available on the market."

Khalid stood up. "Terrific!" he said. "The disease exists, but the medicine for it isn't available." He was about to leave. "You may all be wondering," he said looking at us all, "what's been happening to this particular man. What's his story? Well, you'll find the answer in these prosaic words:

> Innocence in the village,
> Nationalism in the city,
> Revolution in the darkness,
> A chair radiating limitless power,
> A magic eye revealing the truth,
> A living member dying,
> An unseen microbe pulsating with life."

And, with a final "Good-bye," he was gone.

Behind him he left a scene of total confusion. Some people assumed he had been babbling, others that he was actually poking fun at us all, still others that he had been trying to defend himself. He had said that the start had been all innocence and tyrannical forces had corrupted him. But what was the reference to the "magic eye," "a living member dying," and "an unseen microbe pulsating with life"?

A few months later we were all astonished when he showed up again, just like the first time. Why had he come back, we asked ourselves? Why didn't he find somewhere else to wait for his medicine? Did he really want to make his peace with us? Or was there some hidden force pushing him in our direction?

"May I wish you all a very good evening?" he said as he sat down. He looked round. "When God wills that my health improves," he said, "I intend to join your group here."

Munir Ahmad, one of the younger generation who had only joined us recently, asked him why he hadn't explained his little 'prose poem' to us.

"It's self-evident," he replied. "There's no need for explanation. In any case, I hate having to go over all that stuff again!"

"But, Khalid Bey," chimed in Qurunfula, "I have to tell you that your presence here is very upsetting to all of us."

"Nonsense," he replied. "There's nothing like suffering to bring people together."

After a moment's silence, he went on, "I promise you I'll join your little community at the earliest opportunity." He gave a little laugh. "What are you all talking about these days?"

We all thought it best to say nothing.

"I'm well aware of what people are saying," he said. "It's being repeated everywhere. So allow me to clarify for you all the factors in the equation." He adjusted his position on the chair and then continued.

"In our country there are the religious types. Their interest is in seeing religion dominate every aspect of life— philosophy, politics, morality, and economics. They are refusing to surrender or negotiate with the enemy. For them a peaceful solution is only agreeable if it achieves exactly the

93

same result as outright victory. They're calling for a struggle, but what's that supposed to mean? There they all are for you to see, dreaming of prodigious feats of valor performed by the fedayeen or of miracles descending from heaven. They may be willing to accept weapons from the Russians, but all the while they're actually cursing the Russians and insisting that there be no strings attached. Maybe they would prefer an honorable peaceful solution implemented through American intervention since that would put a final end to our relationship with Communist Russia.

"And then there are the Rightists of a particular stripe," he continued. "They want an alliance with America and a severance of all ties with Russia. They would be quite happy with a peaceful solution in spite of all the painful and humiliating concessions we would inevitably have to make. Their dream is to get rid of our current regime and return to a traditional form of democracy and liberal economic policy.

"Next we have the Communists—and the Socialists are essentially a subdivision of the same group. They're interested in just one thing: ideology—strengthening our ties with Russia. They believe that the national interest and progress are best served through ideology, even though the process may involve a very long period of waiting. In consequence, they favor whichever solution anchors the move toward Communism and Russia, whether it's peace, or war, or the current situation which they're calling 'no peace, no war.'"

Remarkable though it may seem, his popularity improved after he had left. Many people valued the survey he had just given and admired his rich store of secret information. Some people even went further and defended the man himself, claiming that he was not the one who was responsible for the crimes he had committed; either that, or else he was not the one primarily responsible.

It was Qurunfula who finally felt compelled to react. "Go on then!" she said angrily. "Shift the blame from one person to the next. It'll finish up with Gum'a, the boot-black!"

However, once Khalid Safwan did decide to join the café community, he found a ready welcome.

⁓

In just three months we forgot all about the person he had been. He used to appear on the arm of his helper at the same time every evening. He would be accorded the same kind of welcome as everyone else; it was almost as though there was absolutely nothing unusual about him. However, he felt somewhat isolated, so he was the one who opened the conversation.

"Are you all still talking?" he inquired, thus intruding on our general disinterest.

"As usual," was Zayn al-'Abidin's reply.

"Earlier I told you about what other groups are thinking these days," he said, continuing his intrusion. "But I haven't told you what I think myself."

"About the war, you mean?" asked Munir Ahmad.

"That seems to be the point that has everyone baffled," he responded in a rush. "To me it seems perfectly simple. We were defeated. We were totally unprepared for war.

That's the problem we have to solve, and quickly, even if it involves paying the price. We should be spending every single penny we have making ourselves more advanced culturally. But I really wanted to talk about our way of life in general."

By now he had everyone's attention.

"In the minutes I have left here," he continued, "I'm going to give you all a frank summary of my experiences. I've emerged from the defeat, or let's say from my past life, strongly believing in a set of principles from which I will never deviate as long as I am alive. So what are those principles?

"Firstly, a total disavowal of autocracy and dictatorship. Secondly, a disavowal of any resort to force or violence. Thirdly, we have to rely on the principles of freedom, public opinion, and respect for our fellow human beings as values needed to foster and advance progress. With them at our disposal it can be achieved. Fourthly, we must learn to accept from Western civilization the value of science and the scientific method, and without any argument. Nothing else should be automatically accepted without a full discussion of our current realities. With that in mind, we should be prepared to get rid of all the fetters that tie us down, whether ancient or modern.

"So there is the philosophy of Khalid Safwan," he said with a yawn. "I've learned its principles from within the deepest recesses of hell. I'm proclaiming it here today in Karnak Café, a place to which we have all been driven by a combination of ostracism and crime."

"Maybe things will turn out better for you and your generation," I said, leaning toward Munir Ahmad.

"There's a huge mound of dirt in our path," he said, "and it's up to us to clear it away."

"Truth to tell," I said sincerely, "your generation—you and your contemporaries—are an unexpected dividend. Out of this all-encompassing darkness a bright light is shining forth, so bright that you might imagine it had been created by magic."

"You don't know what we've been through."

"But we're partners."

He gave me a doubtful stare.

"Tell me," I asked him, "what are you?"

"What do you mean?"

"Which political label best fits you?"

"Damn all such labels!" he replied angrily.

"From your conversation I gather that you respect religion."

"That's true."

"And also that you respect leftist opinions. Is that right?"

"Yes."

"So what are you exactly?"

"I want to be myself, no more, no less."

"Is it a kind of craving for cultural rootedness?" I asked after a pause for thought.

"Could be."

"Does that imply a return to the heritage of the past?"

"Certainly not!"

97

"So where's this 'rootedness' to be found?"

"Here!" he replied pointing to his heart.

Once again I had to pause for thought. "This idea needs further discussion," I said.

"I'm sure it needs a great deal of discussion," he responded in all innocence.

I let the others know how much I admired this young man's vision, to such an extent that one day Zayn al-'Abidin lost his patience.

"Listen," he said. "One day, in two or three years' time, that boy's going to find himself as a civil servant with a miserable salary. That'll leave him with just two choices, no more: corruption or emigration."

That infuriated Qurunfula. "When are you ever going to make a bad mistake," she asked, "and actually say something decent? Just for once!"

"O lovely source of all bounty," he said with a smile of resignation, "the truth is always a bitter pill."

"But there is a third choice," she insisted stubbornly.

"And what might that be, my lady?" he asked humbly.

"Whatever our good Lord chooses!"

I was delighted that she had chosen to react that way. In her case I regarded it as a good sign; perhaps she was now ready to start her life again. However, a new and potentially fascinating idea struck me all of a sudden: could it be, I wondered, that she was beginning to fancy the young man? Was he going to take Hilmi Hamada's place? I'll confess to not being entirely ignorant of the way that some women of her age can behave, how they can feel a passion for adolescent youths and allow folly and adventure to lead them to extremes. I found myself wishing dearly that, if any of the ideas circulating inside my mind were actually to come to pass, the love affair might follow a level path. I hoped that there would be no selfishness on the one side, and no exploitation on the other. The love might once again discover purity and innocence.

Yes indeed, purity and innocence.

♀ Translator's Afterword ♀

Dedicated to the memory of Naguib Mahfouz, great Egyptian, intellectual, and littérateur, humble, warmhearted, and ever-witty individual. Allah yarhamuh.

Readers familiar with Naguib Mahfouz's writings will already be aware of the fact that his works handsomely reward those who are prepared to pay the most careful attention to the nuances of the text. In the case of *Karnak Café*, the English translation of the novel originally entitled *al-Karnak*, this is particularly so, but, in making that suggestion, I am thinking of one very particular instance: the way in which the novel ends. I am not here referring to the much-investigated narratological topic of the strategies employed by novel writers in order to achieve closure, but to the fact that the printed text ends with a reference to the fact that it was completed in December 1971.

A rapid survey of the printed editions of Mahfouz's other novels is sufficient to demonstrate that the author rarely indicates the date of completion in this fashion.

It would appear then that whenever Mahfouz decides to identify dates of composition and completion with such specificity, he has a point to make. So what precisely is that point with reference to *Karnak Café*? The attempt to answer that question takes us conveniently into a discussion of the political context into which it was inserted.

To state that the atmosphere in Egypt in the period after the total defeat in the June War of 1967 was fraught is to indulge in a massive understatement. It was not merely the scale of the defeat and the loss of land that had such an impact on people, but equally, if not more important, the fact that the entire authority structure of the Arab world had been caught red-handed in the act of systematically lying for the entire six-day course of the conflict. In the flash of an eye, triumphal forward marches and victories in the air were turned into abject fiascos. What could be the response, not merely to such a total disaster and loss of precious sons in the Sinai Peninsula, but also to such arrant and deliberate deception? Where now was that national pride engendered by the forward progress of the Egyptian Revolution of 1952? Was it now a case of having to go all the way back to the drawing board? What kind of government could and should now take over the reins of power? What was to be the role and place of the individual? And what was the role of the intellectual, and, more specifically, the novelist?

The post-1967 era was then one of profound dismay, of reflection, of recrimination, of "looking back in anger." The narrator of *Karnak Café* uses a very vivid image to describe the impact of the event: that of a hammer blow crushing the skull. The consequences were, it almost goes without saying, a mixture of utter despair and barely suppressed anger.

Intellectuals responded in different ways. Many writers recorded, either at the time or later, that they felt powerless and totally unable to write anything. Naguib Mahfouz, however, was different. He immediately started writing a whole series of short stories, many of which appeared in his 1969 collection, *Tahta al-mizallah* (some of which are translated in the collection *God's World* [1973]). I mentioned above that Mahfouz pointedly adds a completion date to the text of *Karnak Café*, and it is equally important to note that he inserts in the front material of this short-story collection that they were all composed between October and December 1967; the reference to the aftermath of June 1967 could hardly be clearer. Many of those stories paint a disturbing picture of a world in which no one understands what is happening and, equally important, no one appears to be either in charge or accepting any kind of responsibility. Other stories like these continued to appear in the Egyptian press in 1968 and 1969, and were later published in the collections, *Hikaya bi-la bidaya wa-la nihaya*, and *Shahr al-'asal* (both 1971).

This fraught period in the aftermath of the June 1967 disaster (known in Arabic as *al-naksa* [the setback]) initially saw the resignation of President Gamal 'Abd al-Nasir, the unchallenged figurehead of the Arab world, and then his restitution in the wake of enormous public outpourings demanding that he remain in his post. The toll on his health in the subsequent period was clearly enormous, and he died of a heart attack in 1970 after saying farewell to the Arab leaders who had gathered in Cairo in a vain attempt to formulate a common policy in the face of the crushing new realities. His successor was his longtime vice-president, Anwar (later Muhammad Anwar) Sadat.

I myself can vividly recall the atmosphere in Cairo in the days and months immediately following Sadat's assumption of the presidency of Egypt. The widespread debate on the causes and effects of the June War was still in full swing. To that was now added concern about the new regime and the way in which it would use, and/or react to, the different social, political, and religious elements within the society. One major characteristic of this new era was the encouragement of a disarming level of frankness in describing the 'Abd al-Nasir era, and most particularly the 1960s—they being the prelude to the June 1967 defeat. Naguib Mahfouz himself had been a vigorous participant in discussions concerning the course of the Egyptian revolution since 1952. This was seen most especially in the series of novels that he penned in the 1960s, beginning with *al-Liss wa-l-kilab* (1961; *The Thief and the Dogs*), via the extremely pessimistic vision of *Tharthara fawq al-Nil* (1966; *Adrift on the Nile*), to the most negative of them all, *Miramar* (1967; *Miramar*). What is particularly important to note about these dates and retrospectives refers back to the point I made at the beginning of this short commentary. The December 1971 date makes it clear that this novel belongs firmly to this particular period—the post-1967 period—and debates concerning the course of the revolution and the causes of the defeat to be found within them. This novel is, in a real sense, a continuation of the succession of novels I have just mentioned, those of the 1960s. What is frustrating in this context is that Naguib Mahfouz has left us no reliable record of the sequence of composition of his various works at this period; indeed it appears that there is in effect no 'archive' of Mahfouz manuscripts, since he seems to have deposited most of them with his publisher for printing and not reclaimed the originals—except perhaps in the single case of *Miramar*, of which a manuscript copy appears to exist. That said, we are still left with some clues. I have already drawn attention above to the series of short stories that he wrote in the wake of the June 1967 War, and which, by 1971, had appeared in three book collections. I happened to be in Cairo in the summer of that year and received a telephone call from Mahfouz in which he told me to look out for a new work of his which he was calling *al-Maraya (Mirrors)*; it would, he told me, be a series of vignettes of Egyptian characters, for each of which his friend and colleague, the Alexandrian artist Sayf Wanli, had painted a portrait. Because of the need to publish these portraits in color, Mahfouz had decided to give the initial publication rights for this new work to the television journal *al-Idha'a*. The publication of the series started on May 1, 1971, and continued weekly until the end of September. The book version of *al-Maraya* appeared in 1972 (and the only fully illustrated version of it, along with my English translation, was published by the American University in Cairo Press in 1999). We might therefore suggest that, if Mahfouz had not already started work on *Karnak Café* while penning the episodes of *al-Maraya*, then he started the former work very soon afterward and finished it quickly. What we can surely say—and what a reading of both works readily confirms—is that they both belong to the same period, one involving a retrospective on the period in Egyptian history before and during the 'setback' of June 1967.

All this is of direct relevance to *Karnak Café*, since, unlike the vast majority of his other works, it seems not to have been published in book form within a year, but only appeared in 1974. While I have no documentary proof of what happened to the manuscript in the interim, I would suggest that it is highly likely, bearing in mind the political situation in the early years of the Sadat era, that it was retained either by the author or publisher until the political scenario was somewhat less murky and the serial score-settling of the early 1970s was coming to a close. I have heard it suggested that the version of the novel that appeared in print in 1974 is somewhat shorter than the original text (was there originally, one wonders, a further section in which the narrator interviews Hilmi Hamada, the young Communist, he being the only one of the young trio of habitués at the Karnak Café not to have a section devoted to his opinions and reactions?). As it stands it is in fact one of his shorter novels, but we are unable to say whether that is by design of the author or due to the dictates of censorship or purported judicious omission (and I have been told that the same situation applies to one of the works published before *al-Karnak* but almost certainly written after it, namely *al-Hubb tahta al-matar* [Love in the Rain] [1973]).

The publication date of 1974 for the book version of *Karnak Café* also has to be placed into its proper chronological framework. Much water had flowed under many bridges in Egypt since Anwar Sadat had assumed the presidency. There had been a purge of leftist politicians and an upsurge in the influence of popular religion (the addition of Muhammad at the front of Sadat's official name being merely a prominent symptom of that trend). Many secret memoirs had been published detailing the nefarious activities of various agencies during the 1960s. The Egyptian economy, previously tightly controlled, had been opened up to foreign investment, the so-called 'infitah' policy, which had the major effect of making the rich richer, the poor poorer, and the middle class flounder somewhere in between (all that being a topic on which Mahfouz was to vent a good deal of anger in some of his novels of the 1970s). And, at the Suez Canal, a kind of continuing confrontation between Egyptian forces on the West Bank and Israelis on the East (the Bar-Lev Line) was a thorn in the side of both parties. In October 1973 this stalemate was brought to a sudden end when Egyptian forces crossed the canal (the *'ubur* [crossing]) and managed to breach the Bar-Lev Line. Their advance was soon stopped however, not least as the result of a massive infusion of armaments to Israel from the United States, but, as the French scholar Jacques Berque noted at the time, Egypt had achieved a kind of psychological victory (at least in comparison with the 1967 debacle). Egypt, Sadat, and the armed forces now rode high on a wave of popular celebration; October 6 became then and still is a national holiday, and Sadat, the long-time assistant and subordinate to Gamal 'Abd al-Nasir (and, as such, the butt of many jokes at the time), was now viewed, at least in Egypt and for the time being, as a real national leader.

And that is where *Karnak Café* comes into the picture. For here is a work in which Mahfouz reveals in graphic detail everything that had gone wrong in Egyptian society during the 1960s: the atmosphere of suspicion, the omnipresent eyes of the secret police, the tightest possible controls of press, economy, and culture, and so on. In 1975 a film version of *Karnak Café* appeared, starring one of Egypt's most famous and beautiful movie stars, Su'ad Husni, as Zaynab (she was to die in tragic circumstances in London in 2001). If some of the previous films based on Mahfouz's novels had taken liberties with the storyline and structure of the original work (most notoriously perhaps, in the insertion of an optimistic ending to the film *Miramar*), then this film of *Karnak Café* transcended such practices by a long way, becoming a case of rampant political exploitation. And here is where the gap between the date of completion (1971) of *Karnak* Café and of its publication (1974) becomes crucial. The film proceeds to show the miserable way in which the lives of the young students are impacted and changed during the dire days of the 1960s, but then the 'crossing' of 1973 is introduced into the story as the great turning point that transforms the situation and renders all these nasty moments a part of previous history. I can still vividly remember watching this film in an Egyptian cinema in 1975, with a group of young Egyptian students—disarmingly the same age as the ones depicted in Karnak Café—sitting directly behind me and, as is the norm, commenting out loud on the film as it proceeded. At one point in the film, an army truck is pulled, with disarming inauthenticity, across a stage with a clearly false backdrop behind it, all this intended to represent the Egyptian army going to its destruction in Sinai in 1967 (as fully described in the novel itself). The young folk behind me all assumed that this had to be the '*ubur* (the triumphant 1973 crossing of the Canal) and said so. At that point I probably should have turned round and told them that it was the 1967 defeat and not the 'crossing' and that their sentiments were being shamefully manipulated, but I didn't. Instead it was left to the film itself to show the few stragglers returning beaten and exhausted from the Sinai Peninsula in 1967. Aided by such manipulations, the film had an enormous effect in Sadat's Egypt by casting a massive shadow across the 'Abd al-Nasir presidency; in the commonly used phrase of the time, the rape of Zaynab in prison, or rather the graphic reenactment of it with Su'ad Husni, was regarded as a symbol of the rape of the entire country during the pre-1967 era.

Karnak Café is clearly one of Mahfouz's angriest and most explicit works of fiction. The treatment to which the young people are subjected, the political discussions both before and after the 1967 defeat, and the stark choices facing the Egyptian people in its aftermath, are all portrayed with disarming accuracy. The setting is a café, and one might suggest that, of all the Egyptian authors of fiction whom one might wish to ask to depict the typical café scenario with complete accuracy, Mahfouz is the one who comes to mind first. Apart from his latter years, he loved nothing more than to spend time in cafés, talking with friends and discussing politics and literature. When I first encountered him in the

1960s, his favorite spot was the renowned Café Riche in central Cairo, but both before and after that there were others as well. Indeed another 'story' that I have heard suggests that the advent to Karnak Café of Khalid Safwan is in fact a replication of an actual incident that occurred in a café near the old Opera House.

How ironic is it that Mahfouz puts into the mouth of the villain of this piece, Khalid Safwan, the presentation of the alternatives facing the Egyptian people in the wake of the June 1967 defeat, and indeed places particular stress on the goals of those people who would advocate religion as a basis for finding solutions. One might conclude by suggesting that, while this short novel clearly belongs in and describes a particular chronological context in twentieth-century Egyptian history and social life, the directions that it suggests and the dangers that it identifies make it disarmingly relevant to the situation in Egypt, and the Middle East in general, many years later.

Modern Arabic Literature
from the American University in Cairo Press

Ibrahim Abdel Meguid *Birds of Amber*
No One Sleeps in Alexandria • *The Other Place*
Yahya Taher Abdullah *The Mountain of Green Tea*
Leila Abouzeid *The Last Chapter*
Hamdi Abu Golayyel *Thieves in Retirement*
Yusuf Abu Rayya *Wedding Night*
Ahmed Alaidy *Being Abbas el Abd*
Idris Ali *Dongola: A Novel of Nubia*
Ibrahim Aslan *The Heron* • *Nile Sparrows*
Alaa Al Aswany *The Yacoubian Building*
Fadhil al-Azzawi *The Last of the Angels*
Hala El Badry *A Certain Woman* • *Muntaha*
Salwa Bakr *The Wiles of Men*
Hoda Barakat *Disciples of Passion* • *The Tiller of Waters*
Mourid Barghouti *I Saw Ramallah*
Mohamed El-Bisatie *Clamor of the Lake* • *Houses Behind the Trees*
A Last Glass of Tea • *Over the Bridge*
Mansoura Ez Eldin *Maryam's Maze*
Fathy Ghanem *The Man Who Lost His Shadow*
Randa Ghazy *Dreaming of Palestine*
Gamal al-Ghitani *Zayni Barakat* • *Pyramid Texts*
Tawfiq al-Hakim *The Prison of Life*
Yahya Hakki *The Lamp of Umm Hashim*
Bensalem Himmich *The Polymath* • *The Theocrat*
Taha Hussein *The Days* • *A Man of Letters* • *The Sufferers*
Sonallah Ibrahim *Cairo: From Edge to Edge* • *The Committee* • *Zaat*
Yusuf Idris *City of Love and Ashes*
Denys Johnson-Davies *The AUC Press Book of
Modern Arabic Literature*
Under the Naked Sky: Short Stories from the Arab World
Said al-Kafrawi *The Hill of Gypsies*